The Travail

A Story of Mary and Joseph

By
David M. Worden

PublishAmerica
Baltimore

© 2009 by David M. Worden.
All rights reserved. No part of this book may be reproduced, stored in a retrieval system or transmitted in any form or by any means without the prior written permission of the publishers, except by a reviewer who may quote brief passages in a review to be printed in a newspaper, magazine or journal.

First printing

All characters in this book are fictitious, and any resemblance to real persons, living or dead, is coincidental.

PublishAmerica has allowed this work to remain exactly as the author intended, verbatim, without editorial input.

ISBN: 978-1-4489-7901-1 (softcover)
ISBN: 978-1-4489-6447-5 (hardcover)
PUBLISHED BY PUBLISHAMERICA, LLLP
www.publishamerica.com
Baltimore

Printed in the United States of America

This book is dedicated to my wife, Amanda, and our two children. Without their love, patience and support, this book would never have come to fruition.

The Travail

A Story of Mary and Joseph

My Best To You —

J/M W

12/21/09

Prologue
Antioch, Pisidia

"Where the hell is Bibulus?" Calidus growled, the cold mountain air immediately turning his breath white.

"I believe he mentioned something about his bowels being on fire and ran off into the trees," responded Piso, who was busily setting up his groma[1].

"No doubt too much drink last night. That idiot, if he wants to be an immune[2] this is no way to go about it." On the mountain side behind Calidas the road construction crews were beginning another laborious day of clearing trees and digging trenches, shouts and curses accented by the metallic pings of pick axes echoed off the steep valley walls. A humorless smile crossed Calidus' lips. "Maybe a week spent moving rock and gravel will get his attention. Rullus take the sighting rod and go find Bibulus. Tell that dog to man his post immediately or I swear by the gods that my foot and his arse will collide!"

Rullus soon returned, minus the sighting rod, however Piso could see from his expression that something was wrong.

"You look like you've seen a ghost."

"Rullus, what is it? Where's Bibulus?" Calidus interjected with rising concern.

"Those devils, they tied him to a tree and gutted him like a pig," Rullus replied angrily through clenched teeth.

"Piso, run and tell the officer in charge we may be under attack," Calidus ordered instinctively. "Move it!"

Calidus, drawing his sword, searched the trees and slopes above for signs of movement and steeled himself for the inevitable bloody fight to come.

The Homonadesians had been watching the Roman army construct its road through their homeland for many days and now, on the ridge above the road a small army of men had gathered, hungrily awaiting the signal from their chief to spring an ambush. The Homonadesian chief, silently watching the activity far below, held his arms straight out from his sides, a signal to his men to hold their positions. He knew the purpose of that road; once completed it would allow the Romans to bring their machines of war to within striking distance of his strongholds. His men would be slaughtered; their wives and children would be made slaves. A patient and resourceful man, he had accurately predicted the course of the Roman road which in turn had allowed him to plan and prepare an attack that would have maximum impact with the hope of wreaking havoc and demoralizing the Roman soldiers. He considered himself a lucky man too since the Romans had failed to send out scouting parties and therefore had not discovered his activities. He thought it a strange turn of events but war was like that and the Romans would soon pay for their oversight.

In one fluid move the commander drew his sword and

thrust it downward towards the enemy below. Instantly logs and boulders were loosed from their moorings and began crashing down the mountainside, the thunderous sound all but drowning out the war cries of the warriors racing down the slope on the heels of the avalanche towards the doomed Romans.

* * *

"Unfortunately Saturninus, the Homonadesian cut-throats are not fools," Quirinius said impatiently. "They know better than to challenge us on the open plain. Instead they have chosen to fight us from their mountain strongholds up there on the Pisidian heights. Just this morning a work crew was attacked, over sixty of my men are dead and it will take a week to clear the debris and repair the damaged road."

"I find your tone annoying, Quirinius," Saturninus responded coolly. "Keep in mind I am not one of your officers." Quirinius gave Saturninus a dangerous look but held his tongue. Saturninus continued smoothly, "Are you aware that Caesar has ordered a census of our good King Herod's kingdom; specifically, the provinces of Judea, Idumea and Samaria if I recall correctly?"

"And why should that concern me?" Quirinius said bristling at Saturninus' smugness. "Civil affairs and taxes are your arena."

"You have the only two legions in our part of the world tied up fighting pirates and pillagers! I will need the Fretensis and Gallica Legions to conduct the census, not to mention guard against any kind of rebellion. You know what is happening in Gaul, we do not need that here."

"That puts us in a delicate situation, doesn't it? If we don't handle this correctly I daresay our careers will be over," Quirinius replied in a more conversational tone. "I thought Herod was considered a friend of Caesar's? What happened? Did he fail to pay his tribute?"

"Worse, politics…the Arabian King, Syllaeus, and Herod have been squabbling for some time. Unfortunately for Herod, Syllaeus got to Caesar first and gained his sympathies and so now," Saturninus paused to critique his reflection in a mirror, "Caesar is angry with Herod."

Quirinius thought for moment while he sniffed at a freshly delivered goblet of wine. "Herod is quite a deft politician himself and as unscrupulous as they come. Is he not making an attempt to regain Caesar's favor?"

"He's too sick to travel and is therefore depending on his ambassadors to make his case for him, which reminds me to inform you of yet another complication. Caesar wants to be prepared to take direct control of Herod's kingdom."

"What? Why is that?" Quirinius said bolting upright from his divan and sloshing the contents of his goblet onto his hand.

"Because King Herod has developed a nasty habit of killing his offspring…"

"Hah! That just makes him more Roman than Jew," Quirinius laughed.

"Be that as it may, Caesar believes Herod's unbridled paranoia and his deplorable health are increasingly clouding his judgment. In other words, his ability to rule and to control his subjects is in question." Saturninus smiled slightly, "You may find this amusing my friend, but when Herod put his sons, Alexander and Aristobulus, to death for allegedly plotting against him; Caesar himself remarked that it would be better to be Herod's swine than a son of Herod."

Quirinius rose and walked quietly out onto the balcony and stood for a moment taking in the magnificent view. Antioch stretched out before him; the snow capped Taurus Mountains dominating the horizon. Below him, the banners and battle ribbons of his legions snapped loudly in the freshening breeze.

"I cannot bring the full power of my legions to bear in the narrow confines of these mountains, Saturninus. However, once the Via Sebaste road is completed I will be able to surround and lay siege to these Homonadesians. It will not be long before they will feel the sting of my catapults and ballistae. But it will still take time."

Both men stood quietly as they gazed out at the darkening city below them, the silence broken only by the scurry of house slaves attending to their duties.

"Did Caesar order this census to be done by Romans?" Quirinius asked in a hushed voice as if not wanting to be overheard.

"No, not specifically," Saturninus replied cautiously. Although debating how to follow a decree from Rome was not unfamiliar territory to either of them, there were hazardous consequences to be suffered if results did not meet expectations. "You have devised a plan, perhaps?" he finally prodded.

Quirinius moved closer to Saturninus. "Have Herod conduct the census. He has the resources. We'll tell him his gesture will be looked on favorably by Caesar. As calculating as Herod is, he will no doubt seize the opportunity."

"Yes, yes…," Saturninus nodded enthusiastically. "Very good…" Quirinius' mental agility somewhat surprised him but he was pleased nonetheless. "We'll let Herod deal with any unrest. He's as mean as a snake when he chooses to be. The Jews will no doubt grumble but won't revolt. It'll at the very least buy us time to wrap up your campaign and move our legions back to the south."

Chapter 1

The threshing floor sat deserted and cold, the only remaining evidence of the fall harvest being some scattered piles of rotting chaff. Torrential rains had recently turned the threshing floor to a sea of sticky mud. Overhead, angry looking clouds, remnants of the previous night's storm, were being driven away eastward by a chill wind blowing across the plain.

Beneath a nearby oak tree sat a man, alone except for two sparrows chasing each other through the tree's swaying branches. Despite the gloomy day the man was in a merry frame of mind, in fact he was singing. As he sang the howling wind whipped harder as if attempting to drown out his melodic baritone voice, however he merely sang louder, delighting in the challenge. When his song had finished he rose to his feet and, with a nod to his chirping companions, set out again on his journey. A quick walk down a rocky path brought him to the main road where he turned and headed north.

In the distance the man saw the south ridges of Lebanon rising abruptly out of the Plain of Esdraelon. His excitement grew as the miles trailed away behind him for his final destination lay within those hills. He was carrying a wondrous message, a message that would change mankind forever, the fulfillment of which would bring true justice and peace to all the nations of the world. And it will all start with a humble little girl from a humble little town.

The road rose gently as the plowed fields gave way to sloping vineyards and lofty terraced hills dotted with olive trees. After several miles he turned off the road onto a rutted cart path which wound its way up a steep hillside. Despite the lengthy climb and sharp ascent the man's pace never slackened. At last he topped the hill and there below him, as if hiding from the world, lay the village of Nazareth.

He lifted his bearded face to heaven and shouted, "All praise be to You, Oh Lord!" With a joyful laugh, he burst into song and marched forth down into the village.

Mary peaked out the window and sighed, exasperated. It was still raining; in fact it had been raining hard all morning. She had busied herself preparing the day's bread in hopes that the rain would have let up by the time she finished. She had errands to run, a fact that her mother kept reminding her of loudly.

She sat down in a corner and began rolling yarn, hunkering low so as not to attract her mother's unwanted attention. As always, the dull work allowed her mind to wander and she was soon enjoying the recent memory of her engagement to Joseph. The furrow in her brow relaxed. By this time next year she would be Joseph's wife and Lord willing, she would be pregnant with his son.

Mary had not known Joseph well but what she did know of him pleased her. He had been a friend of her parents for many years and had always treated them with respect and kindness. Her father had long been impressed by Joseph. He had remarked on several occasions that the man possessed a greater share of character and piety than most.

Joseph was gone for long periods of time. His skills as a carpenter and builder were in constant need throughout Herod's kingdom. Though he traveled much, he never failed to visit when he returned home. Mary giggled when it suddenly dawned on her that his visits had become more frequent in the months leading up to their engagement. She fondly remembered the cool nights spent on the roof of her home listening to Joseph regale the family with stories of his travels and the delightfully eccentric characters he had encountered. She loved the way the lamp light would play off his gentle eyes which were set into an elegant but rugged face.

At times the conversations would turn more serious. The Jews were becoming increasingly fed up with Herod's blatant disdain for the Jewish faith and culture and his cozy attitude towards Rome. They were outraged that he was using their taxes to build temples to Roman gods. Joseph whispered that there were even rumblings and stirrings of open revolt. He had heard talk of tearing down the Roman imperial eagle from atop the Temple gate. Joseph felt it was just a matter time now as he shook his head disgustedly. Fortunately he did not dwell long on such matters and would soon return to more pleasant discussions. During her daily trips to the village well she had found herself stopping to admire the houses which she knew Joseph had built. It helped to soothe her heart during his long periods of absence such as now. He was in Jerusalem training the Temple priests to be builders and would not be back for many months.

Mary flinched as the room was suddenly enveloped by a brilliant glow, the piercing light making her head pound. The odd glow faded as quickly as it appeared. Mary got up and hurried to the door wondering if the sun had finally decided to show itself. She peered up at the iron gray clouds and was puzzled since they gave no indication of giving up their blockade of all things blue, bright and cheerful.

Well, at least the rain had stopped Mary thought. She could now get out for awhile and more importantly, away from her monotonous duties and the impatient stares of her mother. She gathered up a tapestry she had woven for one of the wealthier residents of Nazareth and set off quickly, knowing the rain could start again without warning.

Threatening clouds skimmed by just above the trees as she entered the village square. It was normally bustling with activity but today it was empty. The wintry weather had driven all but the heartiest of her fellow villagers indoors.

Navigating her way around the countless puddles of brown water the sound of a beautiful baritone voice caught her attention. Startled, Mary looked up to find a man perched atop a low stone wall enclosing the well, his song of praise to God filling the square. His exceptional voice was complemented by his stunning appearance, his tunic was of the whitest material she had ever seen; his mantel was the color of silver and it shimmered with his every movement. Strangely enough, unlike her sandaled feet, his were completely dry and unsoiled.

Mary typically kept her distance from strangers, she had heard too many times of unwary girls suffering at the hands of a drunken soldier or smooth talking travelers, but she was entranced by this man's appearance and haltingly drew near him.

"Mary, you have come!" the man laughed, his face radiating joy and excitement.

Mary froze, alarmed by the unexpectedly zealous welcome.

"Mary, please do not be frightened," he said as he removed the mantel from his head, revealing hair the color of fire and eyes that sparkled like the Sea of Galilee at sunset.

"You know my name," Mary whispered taking a step back.

"We all know your name, Mary. You are a favored lady for the Lord is with you."

Mary shivered nervously, unsure as to what her reply should be.

"Allow me to introduce myself. I am Gabriel and I have been charged with the wonderful task of delivering a message to you from God."

Mary was sure her legs had gone numb and the act of breathing was becoming increasingly difficult.

"You look as if you will faint. Please, come and sit down." Whether by trust or necessity Mary allowed Gabriel to guide her to the wall. He took off his mantel and spread it across the top of the stone wall for her to sit upon. Once Mary was sitting comfortably Gabriel continued enthusiastically. "God has decided to wonderfully bless you, Mary. Very soon you will become pregnant and have a baby boy. You are to name him Jesus. He shall be very great and he will be called the Son of God. The Lord God will give him the throne of his ancestor David and he will reign over Israel forever. His Kingdom shall have no end!"

Mary shook her head, trying to comprehend the enormity of what she had just heard. This was too much for a simple girl from Nazareth. Her frazzled mind finally seized upon a fact she could understand.

"I am yet a virgin. I have never been with a man so how can I have a baby?"

Gabriel smiled warmly at her innocence. "The Holy Spirit shall come upon you, Mary, and the power of God will overshadow you; so that the baby born to you will be utterly holy—the Son of God. And here is more good news. Six months ago your relative, Elizabeth, the Barren One the people called her, became pregnant."

That was indeed blessed news. Mary had been praying for Elizabeth since she could remember. More than a few times she had overheard her parents speculating about what grave sins Elizabeth must have committed to cause her barrenness.

"This news should help you understand, Mary, that every promise from God will surely come true."

Mary looked up into the sky and sighed heavily. A soft smile formed on her lips. She stood and faced the angel. "Gabriel, I am the Lord's servant and I am willing to do whatever he wants. May everything that you have said come true."

"Peace be with you, Mary."

Mary turned and started for home. It was beginning to drizzle again. She briefly wondered about what she had just gotten herself into. Was she really prepared for this awesome responsibility? As honored and humbled as she felt, she was still a little scared. I will definitely need God's help to get through this, she said out loud just as a little boy ran past, recklessly splashing her with muddy water. She was too lost in thought to notice though. As an after thought she turned to wave at Gabriel only to find him already gone. She did manage to catch a glimpse of a boy on hands and knees, covered in mud. Apparently he had slipped and fallen.

Chapter 2

The evening breeze played with Joseph's black hair while he stared out across the Plain of Esdraelon below. He was gazing southward, his eyes fixed on a plume of dust rising like a pillar from the plain floor. "No doubt another caravan," Joseph mumbled. The company of men and beasts were traveling up the coastal highway, steadfastly plodding their way north to the city of Sepphoris and beyond.

Sepphoris! The very name made his heart ache for that was where his fiancé was living. For how much longer she would remain his fiancé was the vexing question. He was sitting on a hillside overlooking the village of Nazareth and the Plain of Esdraelon, its patchwork of cultivated fields and orchards stretching out before him to the south, east and west. He had ensconced himself in a thick patch of grass beneath an olive tree. It was his favorite hideaway for praying and thinking especially when he was troubled and today he was certainly troubled.

A flickering movement distracted Joseph from his sulking. He looked down in time to see a green lizard nimbly scrambling after a beetle. The lizard easily won the morbid contest. As if to show off its hunting prowess, the lizard scampered quickly past Joseph's feet with the bug hanging out of its mouth.

"At least you are out of your misery," Joseph pouted as he watched the beetle be consumed unceremoniously by the lizard.

With that peculiar diversion concluded, Joseph grudgingly returned to his immediate problem. Mary was pregnant and there was no man to blame, no man to bring charges against. And no man to strangle, Joseph thought irritably as he threw a rock at nothing in particular. What was he supposed to do? The lizard looked on seemingly nonplused.

"Nothing can be easy, can it?" he finally raged out loud at the setting sun, the sudden outburst sending the lizard scurrying, finally ducking into a pile of sticks. Joseph spat angrily and began pacing. He knew he was feeling sorry for himself but, come on? Who had ever had to deal with something like this before? He walked over to a nearby tree and began pounding his head against it. Why him (thud)? Why Mary (thud)?

The day had begun well enough. Joseph remembered how excited he had been returning to Nazareth after his lengthy stay in Jerusalem. He had been commissioned to train Temple priests in the arts of building construction and carpentry. He had worked hard and saved his money in preparation for the wedding. He had even braved the road through Samaria, suffering the insults of the vile and churlish Samaritans in order to get home faster.

Joseph's meeting with Mary's father, Joachim, had proved

to be awkward and disturbing. He had supposed something was not right when he noticed large patches of hair missing from Joachim's head and beard but his premonition had ill prepared him for Joachim's troubling tale. He eventually confessed to Joseph that not long after Mary's return from visiting her cousin Elizabeth, his wife, Anna, noticed a change in Mary's appearance. She knew or rather felt that Mary was with child but couldn't bring herself to face it. When one of Anna's friends made a casual remark about Mary's appearance she could no longer keep silent and conveyed her suspicions to Joachim. With sorrowful hearts they confronted Mary and she admitted to being pregnant.

"But this is not the worst of it," Joachim whimpered as he slumped into a chair. He did not continue as Joseph expected but instead sat trance-like, tearing violently at his beard.

"Please go on," Joseph prompted softly. "I must know."

Joachim looked up at Joseph as if noticing him for the first time. Joachim stared hard at him for what felt like several long agonizing minutes.

"Such blasphemy!" Joachim finally blurted. "I would have rather she had committed adultery."

"Joachim!" Joseph said sternly, his face reddening. "I am losing patience. I myself will rip the hair from your beard if you do not tell me what I need to know."

"All right, Joseph, all right. This is not easy to tell and it will be worse for you to hear. But you are right, as Mary's betrothed it is crucial that you know all. She said an angel visited her and told her that the Holy Spirit would come upon her and that she would then become pregnant with the Son of God."

If Joachim continued speaking Joseph didn't hear it. The

words that kept repeating in his ears were "...the Son of God". He thought he had prepared himself for the worst but those preparations had just now been proved wanting. A cold sweat began springing from his pores as a wave of nausea swept over him. Joseph fell into a nearby chair and remained there motionless and waited for the nausea to pass.

"I must see her," Joseph said after un-sticking his tongue from the roof of his mouth.

"She is living with Anna's family in Sepphoris. You know how the people of Nazareth are?" Joachim said hurriedly in response to Joseph's surprised look. "I was afraid for her life. Sepphoris is a city, a Roman city at that. Up there she is just another Jewish girl."

Joachim was right. Sepphoris and Nazareth were complete opposites. Sepphoris was a bustling, cosmopolitan city perched on top of a tall hill with a commanding view of lower Galilee. It had adopted the Roman culture early on and had become a seat of wealth and influence. And then there was Nazareth, Joseph thought frowning. The few hundred residents of Nazareth lived their lives in a village that was tucked into the hills of lower Galilee, venturing out only to tend their fields and trade a few goods with the passing caravans. They had little patience for foreigners and even less for those who violated Jewish laws. Joseph decided it would be best to hear the story directly from Mary before he made any decisions. Joachim elected to accompany Joseph to Sepphoris. The four mile walk passed in silence.

When Mary entered the room Joseph's heart finally broke. It was one thing to hear she was pregnant; it was quite another to see her. He begged leave of her parents so that they could speak in private. Mary related all that had happened since the angel had appeared to her at the well. She spoke earnestly, without a hint of shame. He winced involuntarily when she quoted the angel saying she would bear the Son of God.

Joseph walked back to Nazareth, his mind completely disoriented. How he had ended up on the hillside he could not remember since he did not recall making the decision to go there. It was as if his feet knew where to go even though he didn't.

Reason and love are two concepts that rarely exist together in life but Joseph did his best to use reason to help him resolve this extraordinary situation. He eventually formulated two acceptable reasons for not taking Mary as his wife. If what she said was true, who was he to raise the Son of God? That honor should go to someone much more worthy than he, perhaps a Levite priest. But if Mary was lying, then he was fully within his rights to end the engagement. But if he didn't marry her, what would become of her? Joseph did not want to cause her any further suffering.

He finally decided to divorce Mary but to do it quietly. Mercy and forgiveness would govern his life, not pride.

It had been a long and trying day and Joseph's head was pounding. He lay down next to an olive tree and was soon asleep.

***

Joseph pulled Mary to him and kissed her deeply. The sweet fragrance of myrrh emanating from the sachet hanging between Mary's breasts enveloped him. The gentle music of a lute caressed the air. After a moment he drew back slowly to drink in her beauty which was as intoxicating as new wine, her raven black hair glimmering like moonlight reflecting off midnight darkened water. With the wedding ceremony concluded, the silent band of well-wishers erupted into a raucous mob, the cacophony of sistrums and timbrels lending fuel to their wine induced exuberance.

As the newlyweds walked up the path an unusually large lizard materialized in front of them, a giant beetle firmly clenched in its jaws. Joseph stopped short at the sight but somehow Mary failed to notice the large beast directly in front of them. The lizard glared at Joseph a moment and then casually sauntered off, the beetle's legs slowly kicking the air.

"That was peculiar," Joseph finally muttered nonplused.

He returned his attention to Mary only to find that her wedding garments were gone. She was now inexplicably draped in her usual garb. When she turned and beckoned to him, he saw that her looks had changed too. She was still lovely but now her face had the softness and fullness of a woman with child.

The people lining the street, who just a minute ago were celebrating, now stood by menacingly, scorn etched into their faces. Joseph, fearing for Mary, tried to quickly catch up with her but slipped and fell on the now muddy path. He attempted to get up but just slipped and fell again. Mary kept on walking, surefooted and steadfast despite the mud. She called to Joseph to hurry but he couldn't get up. And to Joseph's consternation, instead of walking into their home, she turned down a road heading out of the village. He repeatedly tried to call to her but no sound ever left his lips.

"He's waiting on us, we need to hurry" Mary cheerfully called over her shoulder.

Who's waiting on us, Joseph wondered? When he finally lost sight of her, he rolled onto his back and wailed loudly, beat his chest and ripped the wedding garments from his body.

"Get up, Joseph."

"No."

"Joseph!"

"What's the point?"

"Open your eyes. Stop wasting my time."

Joseph peered up through mud caked eyes to see a man with piercing eyes and skin like bronze. He scrambled to his knees and bowed before the man.

"Get up! I am not God, I am only His messenger."

Slowly Joseph rose to his feet, the mud on his skin and garments falling off like scales.

"Joseph, son of David," the angel began, "don't hesitate to take Mary as your wife, for the child within her has been conceived by the Holy Spirit! She will bring forth a Son and you shall name him Jesus, for he will save his people from their sins. This will fulfill God's message through his prophets— The virgin shall conceive a child! She shall give birth to a Son and he shall be called, Emmanuel".

Joseph awoke the next morning just as the eastern sky was beginning to pale. His dew soaked clothes hung limply on his muscular frame. As he shivered in the morning cold he looked down on the cluster of white washed houses of Nazareth…gratuitously mean, close minded and petty Nazareth. While Joseph scratched absently at a new insect bite he noticed an unusually bright star in the morning sky.

Knowing what he had to do, he set out immediately for Sepphoris.

Chapter 3

Joseph rolled a pebble idly from one side of his mouth to the other, lost in thought. It was the Day of Atonement, a time when all Israelites were commanded to go without food and drink from sunset to sunset to atone for their sins against God and each other in accordance with the scripture:

"The Lord said to Moses, "The tenth day of this seventh month is the Day of Atonement; Hold a sacred assembly and deny yourselves, and present an offering made to the Lord by fire. Do no work on that day, because it is the Day of Atonement, when atonement is made for you before the Lord your God."[3] He and Joachim were sitting outside the front door watching the villagers move to and fro as they went about their business. Occasionally one of them would stop and say a few words to Joachim and then move on, completely ignoring Joseph. My donkey is less stubborn than these Galileans, Joseph thought derisively.

He could tell Joachim was anxious because he kept glancing at Joseph nervously. Several times Joseph caught him opening his mouth to speak but then Joachim would just shake his head and look away.

Joseph was pretty certain as to why Joachim was behaving so for he had overheard the muffled arguments between Joachim and his wife, Anna. She was very upset at the thought of Mary leaving so close to her time and insisted to her husband that it would be wiser for Mary to remain in Nazareth until after the baby was born. Anna had repeatedly pleaded with Joachim to speak with Joseph about the matter but up until now he had refused. In fact, as far as Joachim was concerned Mary was now Joseph's problem and he was indeed grateful that they were leaving. However, truth be told, any protest by Joachim would have been in vain anyway. Mary and Joseph were committed to leaving. And yet it was deeper than that. They had never made a decision to leave; they just knew that they were leaving. Registering for the census was a convenient excuse for the curious but the fact was, the Lord was leading them and that was that.

Of course the villagers did not make the thought of leaving difficult. Joseph had quickly grown weary of all the rumors flying about, the one involving Mary and a Roman soldier being the most common. Mary was being shunned by the women of the village and the men, well; they stared at him like serpents sizing up their prey.

Joseph kept his spirits up, happy in the thought that the Son of God would not be born amongst such pathetic and repellant people and that very soon he would be able to shake the dirt of Nazareth from his sandals.

Well, I too am grateful that we are leaving; Joseph thought

defiantly and, casting a final disgusted glance at Joachim, went inside to check on Mary.

Joseph slept fitfully. Worries and frustrations chased each other around his mind and through his dreams all night long. At last the morning dawned, thankfully ending his torment.

As he was loading the packs on the back of the donkey, the donkey swung his head around and butted him.

"Don't start with me!" Joseph growled. This was closely followed by a number of vulgarities and unkindly vows. When his tantrum was over, Joseph felt spent and, not surprisingly, ashamed.

Joseph wandered out behind the stable and raised his eyes to heaven. "Lord, I'm not up to this task," Joseph prayed despondently. "Why did you choose me when there are others so much stronger than I? Mary deserves better."

Joseph leaned on the fence and studied the morning sky, his eyes eventually becoming fixed on a bright star in the east. A sense of calm began to come over him, his panic and frustration slowly evaporating away like a morning mist. He returned to the stable to find his donkey staring at him with watery eyes. He suddenly felt very low.

"Okay, I'm sorry for yelling at you," Joseph said and patted the animal on the neck affectionately. "It seems I can act no better than your kind at times." He exhaled loudly and once again began praying, asking the Lord for wisdom, strength and patience amongst other things. He had a list. It took awhile.

The village was already stirring when Mary and Joseph left. Anna and Joachim saw them off. Anna wept while Joachim stood rigid as a post. Joseph couldn't be sure but he thought he saw a tear forming in Joachim's eye.

They followed the road up out of Nazareth and soon reached the brim of the hill. The view from here was incredible, the clear morning light seeming to magnify the landscape such that Joseph felt as if he could reach out and touch the hillsides of Mount Carmel which dominated the western horizon. Carmel, meaning *fertile ground*, was where Elijah, with the Lord's help, had made fools of the priests of Baal. The priests paid with their lives.

Joseph allowed his eyes to drift eastward, following the outline of the Carmel Mountain range until his gaze fell on Meggido, an ancient city located directly across the plain from Nazareth. In its day, Meggido had been a highly prized city because of its strategic location, sitting astride the only pass through the Carmel Mountains. Through this pass ran the main trade route between Egypt and Mesopotamia, therefore over the years Meggido had become a very prosperous center of commerce. And because this trade route was also the most direct military route between Egypt and Mesopotamia, the city's rulers spared little treasure in their efforts to fortify the city against attack. In fact, it wasn't until the time of King David that Meggido, located within the Promised Land, finally fell to the Israelites. Over the centuries numerous armies had gathered and many a bloody battle had been fought on the plain below the city however now it was not much more than a pile of rubble. Joseph had traveled the road past the city several times during his life. He had always been struck by the eerie silence that hung over the crumbling walls. It was unsettling. On more than one occasion the wind had suddenly picked up and blew hard, violently turning and swirling through the decayed battlements. Joseph believed he had heard voices within the wind, voices of alarm, calling their brethren to arms for a great battle was at hand. These encounters had left Joseph rattled, not because he was afraid of ghosts though. No, what disturbed him was a question these voices begged, were these voices a memory of battles past or a warning of a battle yet to be?

"Joseph, is there something wrong?" Mary asked concerned. Joseph had been so deep in thought that he had lost track of time. A bit embarrassed, he gave Mary a weak smile and shook his head slightly. He then gently prodded the donkey and they began their descent down the hill to the plain below. Neither of them looked back.

The morning was passing uneventfully. They had met a few travelers and gratefully none of them were from Nazareth, Joseph was in no mood to put up with anyone's sneering.

"Joseph, I would like to walk for awhile," Mary said softly as they were passing into the morning shadow cast by Mount Tabor, its sides rising steeply out of the plain.

"Of course Mary, let me help you."

They embraced as Joseph gently lifted her down off of the donkey. The smell of her hair and the touch of her hand on his shoulder sent tingles of warmth through his body. For Joseph, the moment passed much too quickly.

"It hurts my back to ride for so long," Mary said as she leaned backwards, stretching. Her difficulty was very real but it also afforded her a good excuse to walk beside Joseph which was preferable to staring at the back of his head.

He had hardly spoken since leaving Nazareth earlier that morning. Mary's previous attempts at conversation had merely produced a few soft grunts from Joseph. Despite his lack of enthusiasm for talking he had otherwise been touchingly attentive.

She tried again. "So much has happened, Joseph."

Joseph snorted and his somber face stubbornly broke into a toothy smile.

"So much **has** happened Mary. Not so long ago I was returning to Nazareth to prepare for a wedding and now—here we are. I have been thinking and praying all morning. I will have to trust God's plan because I have nothing. I can barely manage getting one foot in front of the other." Mary attempted to step around a pile of animal dung and momentarily lost her balance.

"Hey, you're wobbling a bit," Joseph said as he quickly grabbed Mary's elbow to steady her.

"Sorry, my legs are still a bit stiff. It's not so easy being with child."

Joseph's smile evaporated as quickly as it had appeared, his mood turning serious again.

"Joseph, I will be all right. What is troubling you?"

Joseph would not answer; he just stared down the road as they continued walking. Joseph's awkward silence grieved Mary deeply and tears began forming in her eyes. Why was Joseph here? Was it out of love for her or duty to God? As if to answer her unspoken question, Joseph unexpectedly reached down and clasped her hand gently, the touch of his rough and calloused skin conveying both love and reassurance. Mary leaned into his shoulder and wept quietly. The two walked hand in hand, neither of them taking notice of time or miles passing by.

It was late morning when they reached the western foot of

Mount Gilboa. They had walked many dusty miles during the cool morning hours but with the sun now nearing its zenith, the heat of the day was upon them and it was time to rest. Joseph guided them into a field and found a shaded area that was used by field laborers to escape the afternoon heat. It was a quiet location well away from the busy highway.

Joseph helped Mary dismount from the donkey and steadied her until the numbness eased from her legs. She lightly patted Joseph's hand and set out to find a secluded place to attend to herself. While Mary was gone Joseph busied himself unloading packs from the donkey and building a temporary camp. He spread a blanket on the ground. Then he placed a loaf of bread and a skin of water on the blanket and sat down. Joseph yelped when something sharp stabbed his buttocks. He got up, rubbing his backside, and pulled back the blanket revealing several previously unnoticed jagged rocks. He tossed them aside angrily and laid the blanket out once more. He sat down again but more gingerly this time.

Meanwhile, Mary had found a nook between two young elm trees and settled in for some rest and privacy, removing her sandals and the veil from her hair. She poured some water on her handkerchief and wiped the sweat and dust from her face. A disgusted look crossed her face when she peered down at her feet which were filthy and swollen, the outline of her sandals still impressed into her skin. She washed her feet and rubbed them the best she could. Then she hiked up her tunic to expose her bulbous tummy. She poured a little olive oil on her skin and then lovingly caressed her abdomen, enjoying the moment alone with her baby. The thought of being a mother filled her with a joy that was as deep and wondrous as the sea however worry would occasionally seep in and afflict her mind. Would she be a good mother? Would she be able to protect her baby? What was going to happen to them? As if to reassure Mary, the baby kicked. A tear dropped from her eye and she began singing softly,

"My soul glorifies the Lord,
And my spirit rejoices in God my Savior,
for he has been mindful of the humble state of his servant.
From now on all generations will call me blessed,
for the Mighty One has done great things for me,
holy is his name.
His mercy extends to those who fear him,
from generation to generation.
He has performed mighty deeds with his arm;
he has scattered those who are proud in their inmost thoughts.
He has brought down rulers from their thrones but has lifted up the humble.
He has filled the hungry with good things,
but has sent the rich away empty.
He has helped His servant Israel,
remembering to be merciful to Abraham and to his descendants forever, even as said to our fathers."[4]

Later, after Mary returned, she and Joseph ate quietly and watched caravans and travelers pass by on the road. A hot wind from the east was tossing around the dust kicked up by the camels.

"Why us, Mary?" Joseph abruptly blurted. "We're not

royalty, we're not even Levites. And let's face it, people have little regard for Nazarenes," he said nodding in the direction of Nazareth.

"Come to think of it, I have little regard for Nazarenes—excepting present company of course," Joseph threw in quickly after a dangerous look from Mary.

"I believe the Lord my God cares more about love and honor than status and position," Mary replied. "Maybe we should take heart from the words of our ancestor David. He too considered himself to be insignificant when, despite his sins and shortcomings, the Lord God chose his line to rule over us forever. But his reply was to beseech the Lord to do as he had promised."

"The angel in my dream did address me as, 'Joseph, son of David.' What an unusual greeting? No one has ever referred to me in such a way. I guess the angel was reminding me of my heritage. You're right, Mary. My God is wise and good, and to those he blesses much, he expects much, and what greater blessing could there be than to care for his son?"

Joseph stared up at the slopes of Mount Gilboa while Mary finished nibbling on a fig cake. It was here, he remembered, that King Saul was killed by the Philistine army. Joseph had traveled by this place countless times but had never stopped to consider its significance. Saul had sinned against the Lord and as punishment the Lord abandoned him and directed Samuel to anoint David. Had Saul not been such a fool maybe the Lord would have chosen his line to bless instead. But Saul was a man and men fail. Would he have done any better, Joseph wondered soberly?

Stomachs full and well rested, Mary and Joseph prepared to

break camp. "Do you wish to ride or walk?" Joseph inquired of Mary as she bent to stretch her back.

"Walk. The donkey has enough of a burden."

Joseph patted the donkey's neck. "I'm sure he wouldn't mind, he usually has to carry my tools. Besides, you're not a burden. He's honored to carry you," Joseph added haughtily.

Mary watched the donkey as it patiently chewed on some nearby grass. "His enthusiasm is stirring," Mary teased. "Besides, I'm tired of staring at the back of your head."

The road became busier as the couple approached Scythopolis. Many were traveling to Jerusalem to celebrate the coming holy festival which would begin in a few days. The Feast of Ingathering, a week long celebration that began on the 15th day of Tishri, required that people dwell in booths for seven days as a reminder of the time when the Lord brought Israel out of the land of Egypt and made them live in booths. It was a joyous time of feasting and giving thanks for the bounty of the autumn harvest.

"Who do you think Jesus will be like?" Mary asked squinting up into the bright sky. The sun was beginning its downward trek and the heat of the day was becoming uncomfortable for her. Just then a Roman messenger on horseback thundered past, spurring his horse furiously.

"Maybe he will be like David and unite us in driving these Romans from our land," Mary continued, waving dust away from her face.

"You pose an exciting question, Mary. The possibilities are endless. My thoughts are that first he will need to lead us back to God. Our people have strayed terribly. We have stopped trusting God. That is why the Romans are here." Joseph related to Mary the story of how the Hasmoneans had rid the land of the Seleucids but in their arrogance they started proclaiming themselves to be both kings and priests. This would be their downfall for the scripture says that kings can only come from the tribe of Judah and priests from the tribe of Levi.

"They should've known better. Hadn't Saul committed the same crime?" Joseph asked in an exasperated tone. "Well, it wasn't long before brother turned against brother and all the while their lust for power was blinding them to their sin. Finally, in desperation, Hyrcanus conspired with Rome to help him crush his brother, Aristobulos. The Romans have been here ever since. Rome did not conquer us, our sin did."

"Then how will Jesus lead our people back to God if he first doesn't become king? Do you think Herod will just abdicate the throne?" Mary asked innocently. "He's a Jew. He should be familiar with the prophecies, shouldn't he?"

"Herod is a half-Jew," Joseph replied with disgust. "Actually he is Idumean. His family was forced to convert to Judaism. He goes through the motions but that's about it. Actually Mary, let's hope he is *not* familiar with the prophecies. Herod is a brutal and paranoid man, he suspects treachery around every corner and his secret police are everywhere. He murdered his own wife and sons to protect his throne."

Joseph had to stop himself for he could see he was scaring Mary and so he left his final thought unsaid which was, if Herod was to ever find out about them he would surely have them killed.

Mary stared in shock at Joseph. "How did we end up with such a man?" she asked as tears began falling from her eyes.

Joseph held her close as Mary buried her face in his neck and wept. While he stroked her hair he remembered the haunting warning of Samuel to the people of Israel when they rejected God as their king and instead wanted an earthly king. Samuel admonished them,

"This is what the king who will reign over you will do: He will take your sons and make them serve with his chariots and horses, and they will run in front of his chariots. Some he will assign to be commanders of thousands and commanders of fifties, and others to plow his ground and reap his harvest, and still others to make weapons of war and equipment for his chariots.

He will take your daughters to be perfumers and cooks and bakers.

He will take the best of your fields and vineyards and olive groves and give them to his attendants.

He will take a tenth of your grain and of your vintage and give it to his officials and attendants.

Your menservants and maidservants and the best of your cattle and donkeys he will take for his own use.

He will take a tenth of your flocks, and you yourselves will become his slaves.

When that day comes, you will cry out for relief from the king you have chosen, and the Lord will not answer you in that day."[5]

Joseph was furious with himself for needlessly upsetting Mary. He hugged her lovingly and lifted her onto the donkey. "Forgive me, Mary," Joseph said looking into her beautiful brown eyes. "My tongue wags too much at times."

The two spent the night on the outskirts of Scythopolis, a

Roman city that was built in the valley just below the ancient Israelite city of Bethshan which, Joseph remembered, was where the Philistines brought the headless bodies of King Saul and his sons and nailed them to the city's wall. Scythopolis was beautiful, possessing a colonnaded main street, bath houses and a large amphitheater. However it was also home to many pagan temples and therefore the Jewish couple loathed the thought of entering such a city.

Joseph woke early, just before dawn. They had another long day of travel ahead of them but he didn't have the heart to wake Mary just yet. He watched her tenderly as she lay deep in slumber. It's ironic, Joseph thought, that the wish of every Jewish maiden was to be the mother of the coming Messiah however when the miracle occurs, the poor girl is ostracized.

As disturbing as recent events had been Joseph couldn't help but be heartened by Mary's fierce faith. She knew what could happen to a girl that becomes pregnant before marriage. The town turned on her; even her friends abandoned her, but she remained resolute in her faith; sure that God's plan would be carried out through her. And now, at the height of her pregnancy she had to undertake the long, and not so safe, road to Jerusalem. Joseph stroked her hair softly and then yielding to duty, rose to begin packing. He quietly assembled the packs and headed outside. He paused in the doorway, looking out into the dark morning sky.

"A bit tough, aren't you?" Joseph muttered glancing upward. He blushed suddenly when Mary replied sleepily, "Me or the donkey?"

Busy loading their packs on the donkey, Joseph was not aware of the stranger silently approaching from behind.

"You are Joseph of Nazareth." It was a woman's voice. Joseph turned quickly to see the figure of woman standing a few yards away. Even in the morning light, as meager as it was, he could still distinguish her painted features and that she was dressed in crimson robes, garlanded with gold chains.

He remained silent, not sure how to respond. She had spoken his name not so much in a statement of fact, but in an almost accusatory way.

"No point in denying it, I know you are he and I know where you're bound," she continued impatiently.

"How do you know these things?" Joseph replied, eying the woman suspiciously and purposefully admitting to nothing.

"I have the ability to commune with spirits, they tell me about events that have not yet happened," she responded proudly.

"That is a sin, woman!" Joseph retorted angrily.

"A sin? Hah! It is a gift, a gift from the gods and one that has made my master very wealthy," she fired back. "And as you can see," the woman continued in a softer tone and stroking her fingers across her gold necklaces, "He rewards me handsomely."

"I want nothing to do with you. Be gone!"

"Don't be so quick to dismiss me, Joseph. I was sent here by my master to help you."

"Who is your master?"

"He goes by many names but there is no time to run down the list. Let's just say he knows of your predicament and wishes to help."

"To what predicament are you alluding? Speak plainly."

The woman sauntered forward, a knowing smile upon her

face, her flowery perfume momentarily distracting Joseph. "Your wife Mary is carrying the son of a god, is she not? Yes, the spirits know about Mary," she added, relishing the distressed look upon Joseph's face.

"Wha'-, what would your master have me do?" Joseph asked, almost in a whisper. Rather than answer the woman strolled past him, eyeing him, and began scratching the donkey under his chin. Clearly, Joseph thought, he was at a disadvantage and she knew it.

"Turn back, Joseph of Nazareth," she said languidly. "It's that simple."

"I can't do…"

"You must," the woman interrupted, her casual tone gone. "If you go back you will be blessed with many sons, you will grow old comfortably and be held in the highest regard."

"And if I choose not to—?"

"The spirits warn of indescribable suffering, privation, violence and death. You're a good man Joseph. You wouldn't knowingly endanger your family?" she implored, mustering a well rehearsed pouty face.

Her question struck him like a hammer. What man *would* knowingly endanger his family? Leaving Nazareth just seemed like the right thing to do but Gabriel, God's messenger, never instructed them to leave. Was he following God's plan or his own?

The woman could see that her words were having the desired effect on Joseph, her confidence bolstered by her master's promise of the gold and jewels that would be bestowed upon her if she could convince Joseph to return to Nazareth. But what if the unthinkable happened? What if she failed? Well, that line of thinking would have to wait till later. As gracious as her master was, he sometimes just expected too much and this was one of those times. He had been very insistent concerning this man from Nazareth, for what reason he would not divulge.

The necromancer did not like this. She had a gift which allowed her to see the unseen using her spirits; and she cared not what individuals did with the information she provided so the sooner she could be rid of this peasant, the better.

Joseph watched the woman impatiently shift her weight from foot to foot. He also noticed that she was no longer gently scratching the donkey under the chin but raking her long painted finger nails across his cheek. Tufts of hair were beginning to pile up on the dirt below.

"I don't know you or your master," Joseph finally replied. "Your words may be truthful but I have no way of knowing and to be honest, I don't trust you."

"Be wise Joseph, think of your family," the woman responded desperately. "You must go back!"

"I will let God choose my path for it is written that it is better to trust in the Lord than to put confidence in man."

"You're a fool, Joseph of Nazareth!" Just then the donkey sneezed, spraying mucus all over the woman's crimson robes and her sandaled feet.

"To hell with you," she shrieked as she ran past Joseph. He watched her until she passed out of sight and then turned and gave the donkey a reproving look.

"You did that on purpose, didn't you?" Joseph said, allowing a hint of humor into his tone. In response, the animal swished his tail happily.

THE TRAVAIL

Between having to ford the river Jordan and the ever growing number of travelers on the road, progress had become slow and Joseph was increasingly concerned that they wouldn't be able to find suitable shelter. He worried that Mary could have this baby at any time.

He had intended to arrive in Jerusalem well ahead of the festival in order to be assured of finding a room for Mary because, Joseph thought, it was only fitting for the Son of God to be born in Jerusalem, the holiest of cities.

But Joseph chose not to disturb Mary with his concerns, she had enough to deal with, more accurately she had dealt with too much already. Mary had recounted to him what had happened, often through tears, when she had returned from her visit with her cousin Elizabeth. She had been so full of joy but when she told her parents about her encounter with the angel and that she was now pregnant her parents refused to believe her. Worse yet, they accused her of blasphemy and bringing immeasurable shame on the family.

The only thing her father did for her was to protect her from the villagers. He warned the Nazarenes that Joseph, her fiancé, had the final decision, not them.

So her father had spirited her away to Sepphoris where Mary spent her time alone in a house, shunned by friends and family alike until that day Joseph returned.

Travel to Jerusalem prior to a festival was always heavy but because of the Roman census there were more travelers than usual. The Romans had picked a good time to carry out their census, between the fall harvest and the onset of the winter rains. Also, with Jerusalem being the largest city, it made it even more convenient to get people registered since they were going to Jerusalem anyway.

It was convenient for everyone except Mary and Joseph. Forcing Mary to travel from Nazareth to Jerusalem was not Joseph's preference for Mary was in her final month of pregnancy and traveling that great a distance was the last thing she needed. The road was inherently dangerous—bandits, wild animals, and biting insects were a constant threat.

But Joseph and Mary knew that staying in Nazareth would have been worse. Even after he had accepted Mary as his wife he knew those contemptible people would never stop in their harassment. Joseph determined that the Son of God would not be born in such a pathetic place; they would start a new life in the south where no one knew them and because of Herod, there was plenty of work for a carpenter in Jerusalem.

Chapter 4

"It's hot, dusty and desolate. Jericho can't be too much farther," Joseph said, making a weak attempt at humor. Mary did not respond for fear of being unnecessarily rude, the harsh sun having put her in a foul mood. Her spirits were soon lifted though when the city of Jericho did finally come into view a few miles west across a narrow plain, lying against the bleak Judean hills.

Jericho reminded Mary of an emerald, the green lush gardens and numerous orchards making the city stand out in stark contrast to the surrounding inhospitable countryside. She could just make out King Herod's palace, its intimidating fortifications rising above the city's walls to the south.

Jericho was one of the oldest and wealthiest cities in the land. It sat along side the major road that carried trade between the Kings Highway and Jerusalem. Its thirsty orchards were fed by local springs and aqueducts delivered water from the mountains to the west. Also, sitting at 800 feet below sea level, Jericho was typically hotter than the surrounding country which is why it made for a comfortable winter residence for the king.

Much had happened during her long history. It was the first city conquered by Joshua when the Israelites entered the Promised Land. King David escaped to Jericho when his son Absalom attempted to overthrow and kill him. And to punish King Herod for resisting her advances, Cleopatra of Egypt had once persuaded Marc Antony to give her the district of Jericho with its world renowned balsam plantations and date palm trees.

It was here too that the Chaldean cavalry ran down and captured King Zedekiah, the last king of Judah, and his men thus bringing his ill conceived rebellion against King Nebuchadnezzar of Babylon to an ignominious end. Zedekiah was shackled by his captors within sight of the river Jordan and dragged away to Riblah in chains where he died in captivity.

Joseph carried Mary across the river ford and then went back for the donkey. They were now in Judea. It had become increasingly humid as they approached Jericho and the heat remained stifling. At least they could now escape the harsh sun in the shade of the orchard trees. While Joseph went in search of a room, Mary rested against a tree, thankful to be off her feet. Despite her physical discomfort in her heart she was gleeful. She had trusted in the Lord and he had not failed her.

Mary watched Joseph until he disappeared behind a caravan of dromedaries. A large family making camp nearby caught her attention. When they had finished the father sat down and beckoned his many children to his side. He began singing what apparently was his favorite psalm. He was a large man with an unexpectedly sweet voice and laughing eyes. He sang his psalm with great zeal and moved his arms animatedly with the rise and fall of his voice. It was a song Mary had heard before. She heard him sing,

"Sons are a heritage from the Lord,
children a reward from him.
Like arrows in the hands of a warrior are sons born in one's youth.
Blessed is the man whose quiver is full of them.
They will not be put to shame when they contend with their enemies at the gate."[6]

When he finished he spread his arms wide, an action which the children took as an invitation to immediately rush at him, practically bowling him over. Mary laughed as she watched the children dance around their father. The sound of her laughter caught the attention of the man's wife who was sitting quietly off to the side holding a baby. She smiled kindly and nodded to Mary.

She closed her eyes and began praying, thanking God for sending Joseph to her. She felt sorry for what he had been through, returning to Nazareth to prepare for their wedding ceremony only to walk into a hornets nest. Angry gossip had then consumed the tiny village, some thinking Joseph had gotten Mary pregnant while others thought she had committed adultery.

"A bit tough, aren't you?" Mary said softly staring up through the tree branches.

"Me or the donkey?" Joseph had to duck when Mary playfully flung a rock at him.

Joseph told Mary he had found them a room although he

reckoned that up until several days ago, it had been no more than a sheep stall. In fact, it stilled smelled of its previous occupant despite the fresh straw.

"You never did tell me about what happened to Zechariah, your cousin Elizabeth's husband," Joseph said, flinging away a small stick he had been chewing on. "Why was he struck dumb?"

"It's a good story of faith," Mary said. "Or more accurately, a lack of faith," she continued with a twinkle in her eye.

It was dawn; Zechariah entered the temple area from the outer courts, carrying a magrephah, a small gong, which he struck repeatedly as he walked. Levites and worshippers gathered round and followed him to the sanctuary. Before entering the sanctuary, two other priests joined him at his sides and the three passed through the entrance together.

The golden altar, standing three feet high and 18 inches square, was immediately before them. Behind the altar was a huge thick curtain, and behind the curtain was the Holy of Holies. The only light in the room was provided by a fire burning atop the golden lamp-stand.

One of the priests went forward and placed burning coals on the altar. Once his task was completed the other priest then went forward and arranged the incense on the table so that it would be ready to add to the coals. The two priests then left thus leaving Zechariah alone and not a little scared.

He had been memorizing a prayer for some time in hopes he would one day be the incense priest. He wanted his prayer to be worthy of this awesome and once in a lifetime opportunity. He shut his eyes and ignoring the flutter in his stomach, concentrated on offering up his prayer.

Unexpectedly, the room grew bright and despite having his eyes closed, Zechariah' eyes stung horribly. The light quickly dimmed however and Zechariah reluctantly opened his eyes. He scanned the room from left to right, his eyes watering heavily. He was shocked to spot the outline of a man standing to the right of the altar.

Fear swiftly fell upon Zechariah. No one could have entered this room; the doors were guarded by his fellow priests. This could not be a man.

"Do not be afraid, Zechariah, for your prayer is heard," the angel said to him in a warm and comforting voice.

"You must be an angel," Zechariah interrupted, his words forming slowly because his tongue refused to cooperate. "Since no man would dare violate the law," he continued almost soundlessly, not intending for the angel to hear.

"I have a message for you from the Lord. Now be still and listen. Your wife Elizabeth will bear you a son, and you shall call his name John. You will have joy and gladness, and many will rejoice at his birth."

The angel paused to see if Zechariah wished to say anything. He didn't, so the angel continued, "He will be great in the sight of the Lord, and shall drink neither wine nor strong drink. He will also be filled with the Holy Spirit, even from his mother's womb. And he will turn many of the children of Israel to the Lord their God. He will also go before Him in the spirit and power of Elijah, to turn the hearts of the fathers to the children, and the disobedient to the wisdom of the just, to make ready a people prepared for the Lord."

The angel looked at Zechariah expectantly, pleased that he

could finally deliver this message and that they could now praise the Lord together. It was not to be so.

"How shall I know this?" Zechariah asked petulantly. "I am an old man, and my wife is well advanced in years."

Angry, the angel stepped towards Zechariah, who immediately retreated, and answered him saying, "I am Gabriel, who stands in the presence of God, and was sent to speak to you and bring these glad tidings. And now you want a sign to prove what I tell you? Do you really think you were chosen by lot? You prayed for many years for a son, and in spite of Elizabeth's barrenness, you remained faithful and loving to her. You never once considered divorcing her. And here, at the moment of truth you choose to allow your faith to fail? You irritant! Behold, you will be mute and not able to speak until the day these things take place, because you did not believe my words which will be fulfilled in their own time."

Joseph ran his hands through his hair, laughing in disbelief. "Zechariah is a priest and yet he forgets so easily the story of Abraham and Sarah."

"You should not judge so harshly," Mary reprimanded. "We are all tested at times. By God's grace alone are our failings forgiven."

"I agree," Joseph said, backing down. "But still, to argue with an angel—?"

Chapter 5

Mary and Joseph sat quietly eating, watching the sun dip behind the Judean Hills. The sweltering heat of the day was stubbornly giving way to the cool of the desert evening. Around them were groups of pilgrims who, seemingly as one, began packing rucksacks and loading packs on their assorted beasts of burden. Mary and Joseph did the same and promptly fell in with one of the several large groups of faithful to begin the long and daunting climb from Jericho to Jerusalem.

This was the last leg of their journey, only fifteen miles; however this was also the most dangerous part. Known as the "Ascent of Blood", the road between Jericho and Jerusalem was frequented by bandits. Even wild animals were known to attack the unwary soul traveling alone. Add to this the fact that Jerusalem was 3000 feet higher in elevation than Jericho; this trek across the wilderness presented a mighty challenge for even the fittest youth.

The pilgrims began their journey happily enough, singing Songs of Ascents as they passed beneath the limestone walls of

King Herod's winter palace, its ornate works reflecting the light of countless torches. The songs continued as the group followed the road as it tracked between the two hilltop fortresses of Cypros and Taurus, the moonlight making them to appear as two unblinking eyes.

The reassuring lights of the city grew fainter as the band of faithful trudged its way into the wilderness and were soon out of sight of even the hilltop fortresses. The merry songs died away to muted whispers and owing to the constraints of the narrow road the people could no longer travel as one group but had to continue on in single file. Overtime the young men moved out ahead of everyone else while the elderly and those with young families fell farther behind and before long Joseph and Mary found themselves alone although from time to time they would catch a glimpse of a small group in the distance ahead of them.

This was not Joseph's first time on this particular road but it was the first time where others were in his charge. The responsibility that God laid on his shoulders weighed heavily on him and Joseph worried he was not up to the task. He turned to look back at Mary as she gently swayed in rhythm with the donkey's gate.

"I'm all right Joseph," she whispered.

"We'll be coming to a spring soon. We can stop and rest there for a few minutes," Joseph stated authoritatively in order to hide his foreboding.

To ease his apprehension Joseph racked his memory for an appropriate psalm. Not surprisingly this song of David came quickly to mind. Joseph chanted,

THE TRAVAIL

"The L<small>ORD</small> is my shepherd; I shall not want.
He maketh me to lie down in green pastures:
he leadeth me beside the still waters. He restoreth my soul:
he leadeth me in the paths of righteousness
for his name's sake.
Yea, though I walk through the valley of the shadow of death, I will fear no evil:
for thou art with me;
thy rod and thy staff they comfort me.
Thou preparest a table before me
in the presence of mine enemies:
thou anointest my head with oil;
my cup runneth over.
Surely goodness and mercy shall follow me
all the days of my life:
and I will dwell in the house of the L<small>ORD</small> for ever."[7]

The road narrowed to a rocky trail as it turned to the left and dipped down into a shallow ravine. They followed the dry stream bed for a short while. Joseph thought the spring should be coming up soon, just past where the ravine bent northward. Snorting loudly, the donkey abruptly stopped and reared back, nearly yanking Joseph off his feet. Hair standing on end, the donkey bounced its head up and down and brayed noisily. Joseph moved quickly to gain control of the animal fearing Mary would be bucked to the ground.

From up ahead a muffled shriek split the air, its echoes continuing down the rocky ravine. Angry shouts and pleas for mercy soon followed. Joseph lifted Mary off the panicked donkey and hurriedly escorted Mary back down the trail and hid her in a small grotto. Satisfied she would be safe at least temporarily, he returned up the trail and retrieved his adze from a pack on the donkey's back.

Joseph moved forward warily, using boulders and brush as cover. The cries and shouts continued but were becoming fainter and, Joseph felt, different somehow. They sounded more like the cries of panicked soldiers fleeing before a merciless enemy. Despite the chilly desert breeze flowing down the ravine, Joseph was drenched in sweat. He leaned against the foot of the rock cliff while he caught his breath and planned his next move. This is just perfect, Joseph muttered to himself. It's dark; I'm in unfamiliar territory with an unknown danger ahead of me. A loud moan off to his right sent him diving into a patch of tall grass, the coarse blades scraping against his arms and neck. Joseph lay still listening but other than the sound of his beating heart in his ears, the quiet of the night was undisturbed. He rolled lightly onto his side and suddenly screamed. He was face to face with a dead man. The bearded face appeared ghostly white in the remaining moon light and by the look of the man's eyes the wretch had died screaming in terror.

"Stay back," cried an anguished female voice. Joseph slowly stood, his adze held out before him.

"Who are you?" Joseph hissed.

"My husband is dying and you have already taken all we have. Go!"

"Woman, I am no thief," Joseph said, lowering his weapon and stepping closer. He could now clearly see a woman kneeling on the ground with her husband's head in her lap.

"What is wrong? Is he bleeding?" Joseph said as he knelt next to the man.

"He seems to have several cuts on his head. I saw one of the bandits hit him in the head with a heavy club," the woman said trying hard not to cry. "He fought them, he is a strong man but there were many of them."

"Is it just you two here? Anybody else hurt?"

"Only our children. See? They are returning."

Joseph looked up to see what seemed like a small army of shadows moving towards him. They came out from behind rocks, bushes and several even climbed down off the low ravine cliffs. The last to show up was a tall girl carrying a baby that was crying weakly. "I told them to run when the bandits came upon us. One threw me harshly to the ground which is when my husband set into them."

"You are fortunate to be alive. These men have no pity."

"Something drove them off. I thought soldiers were coming."

"I must go fetch my wife and our supplies," said Joseph. "I will return shortly."

"I am here." He turned to see Mary approaching, the donkey obediently following along behind her. "I heard the crying baby and then spotted the girl walking up the ravine. So I followed her."

Joseph shook his head, at once angry with her for placing herself in danger but yet grateful for her presence. He got up, hugged his wife briefly and started unpacking one of his satchels. "Woman, if you have any lamps, we will need them."

"I do not know what we have anymore. Our belongings are scattered everywhere and our donkey is gone." The woman turned to her children, "Boys! Go and find what you can and bring it back here. Do not stray too far though, there is still danger about." Mary and Joseph watched as the grey shapes of the children moved off into the dark.

Joseph removed a satchel from his donkey and carried it over and set it down next to the injured man. He brought out his lamp and a flask of oil. After a few long minutes he managed to light a small fire and then used the flame to light the oil lamp. He held the lamp aloft while moving it up and down the man's body and taking note of his wounds. He was unconscious, only the occasional groan providing any indication he was still alive. The man indeed had several cuts on his head, one above his left ear and the other across his nose and cheek. One eye had swollen shut. There were some smaller cuts on his forearms with the exception of one particularly deep gash where the flesh had been laid open. Joseph lifted the man's tunic and found deep bruising along his ribs.

Up until now the woman holding her husband's head had been surprisingly stoic but the sight of his awful injuries and his blood that now stained her own hands was just too much. She broke down sobbing, her whole body quaking as tears poured off her cheeks and on to her husband's bruised and distorted face.

The baby was becoming increasing fretful, its cries more demanding. Mary, with tears in her own eyes, stepped forward and gently placed her hand on the woman's shoulder. She knelt next to her and whispered soothingly in her ear, hugging her closely.

"What is your name my dear?" Mary asked.

The woman turned her face up towards Mary. "It is Rebecca

and," she said while stroking the man's hair, "this is my husband, Samuel." Mary breathed in sharply for she knew this woman. She was the mother from the family that Mary had watched with so much joy back in Jericho.

Despite the efforts of Rebecca's eldest daughter, the baby continued to cry pitifully. The little boy just wanted his mother. Mary, knowing Rebecca was in no condition to care for the baby asked if she could hold the baby. Rebecca nodded wearily.

Mary walked over to the girl and held out her arms. "May I?" The anxious girl gave the baby up to Mary who then immediately embraced the child and began caressing his cheek. The baby fell silent and began gently cooing as he stared up into Mary's face.

"Our stuff has been flung all over," said a young boy, about ten years of age Joseph thought, who had quietly appeared at his mom's side. "We are gathering together what we can find in the dark. Simon has found our donkey, it was just a little ways up over there," the boy stated excitedly as he waved his hand in a generally northward direction.

"Thank you Malachi, don't be much longer," Rebecca called after him as he scampered off.

Joseph worked quickly, calling on all his skills to help Samuel. He bathed the man's wounds in water from the spring which was being brought to him by several of Rebecca's daughters in a variety of containers, essentially whatever they could find under the circumstances. He applied honey to the open wounds and bound them tightly in strips of cloth.

"Rebecca," Joseph said as he sat back, exhausted, "the good news is that Samuel is not dying but he will need a physician.

The bad news is that none of us can lift such a big man. We will need to wake him and see if he can walk under his own power. If nothing else maybe we can get him mounted on your donkey."

"The way you were working I thought you were a physician."

"No, I am a builder but we tend to hurt ourselves," Joseph chuckled lightly.

"You have shown us tremendous kindness, both you and your wife. May God grant many blessings to you, um, forgive me, what are your names?"

"My wife's name is Mary and I am Joseph, we are from Nazareth."

"Mary and Joseph, I recognize you now. I saw you back in that orchard in Jericho. And Mary, you are with child. By the looks of it your time will be very soon. You two must leave at once," Rebecca said urgently. "This is no place to give birth!"

"We cannot just leave you here, besides who will help with your husband?" replied Joseph.

"No, you must go. I have nine children," Rebecca said proudly. "They will help."

"And a heartier and braver bunch is not to be found," Joseph said sincerely. "But I insist we stay, at least until morning. It has been a difficult night and you must tend to your husband. I will keep watch. Remember, you need to wake him but do not let him move around. Give him as much water as he can stand." With that said Joseph left to round up the boys.

Rebecca let go with a loud sigh. "Is he always that stubborn?"

"Pretty much," Mary nodded.

THE TRAVAIL

"My Samuel, too. God has blessed you in so many ways."

"You have no idea."

Joseph soon found Simon as he was leading the donkey back to the spring. He told him to gather up his brothers and sisters and return to the spring and stay there. He further instructed him to unpack the donkey for it would be needed to carry his father. Simon politely questioned Joseph as to the well being of his father.

"He is hurt, yes, but he is a strong man and with the help of an able son like you he will be just fine."

Buoyed by Joseph's confidence Simon headed for the spring but stopped suddenly. "Joseph, There are several dead men out there. I don't understand. Who killed them?"

"Maybe those wicked scoundrels turned on each other," Joseph shrugged. "I'll take a look."

Sure enough, as Joseph patrolled the rest of the night he came upon at least seven dead bandits. The beasts of the desert will feast well, Joseph thought. He turned to look eastward. The ravine walls were sharpening against the horizon. Dawn was coming and there again was that unusually bright star in the morning sky. He headed back to join the others.

Joseph walked up in time to see a number of the younger children gathered around their father. He thought he heard them laughing and then he saw that Samuel was sitting up and hugging his children one by one.

"You should not be moving so much, those bandages are not to be trusted," admonished Joseph.

"Ah, Joseph," Samuel bellowed with unexpected strength. "My Rebecca tells me I have you and your wife to thank for saving my life."

"No, my friend, God is to thank. We were merely the instruments of His mercy," Joseph replied humbly.

"Then we shall glorify God together." Samuel paused and stared hard at Joseph. He finally continued. "Tell me though Joseph, are you a prince?"

"No," Joseph replied startled at the question.

"A captain then?"

"No, Samuel. I am Joseph of Nazareth. A builder."

"Interesting, this is interesting. You see, Joseph, these men," Samuel said gesturing at the dead attackers, "they were all set to finish me off when we all heard the thunder of many horses. The ground shook, my friend. Before I passed out I saw soldiers approaching swiftly from over there. There were even chariots. At first I thought it was patrol of Roman soldiers but their armor—it was like none I had ever seen, it was luminous. Even the horses shone with a bluish hue. These two men here were struck down right in front of me—the rest fled.

"I thought you had killed them," Joseph said looking over at Rebecca who merely shook her head.

"Sir, I am no warrior. Those dogs did not fall by my hand."

Daybreak came and went. It was decided that Samuel and Rebecca should return to Jericho since it was the shorter and easier road. They would also be more likely to encounter a Roman patrol and get some help. Joseph, with the help of Samuel's older sons successfully mounted Samuel on the family's donkey. It was a grueling undertaking and at times comical with Samuel stumbling and lurching about, arguing the whole time that he was perfectly capable of walking.

Joseph and Mary started for Jerusalem. He steered clear of the dead bodies strewn about the ravine floor but the stench could not be avoided. It hung in the air like a foul morning mist and the putrid smell caused Mary to get sick more than a few times. During one of those unfortunate incidences, Joseph, while standing by and comforting Mary, was suddenly distracted by a whimpering sound. He couldn't be sure if it was coming from a wild animal or a wild man; perhaps lurking in one of the many caves along the rock wall. Either way Joseph knew they needed to move along quickly. He knew his pregnant wife was miserable but there was a need for haste. The donkey apparently agreed with Joseph's analysis of the situation because it did not protest the quickened pace.

The caves stank of sweat and urine. The gang's refuge had now become its prison. Hunger and thirst descended on them like vultures, the agony intensified by the knowledge that sweet water lay only a few hundred feet distant. As the night wore on the distraught bandits drew away from each other, becoming encapsulated in their own cocoons of misery. Some cursed, some cried while others sat rocking on their haunches and stared at nothing. One of their number, evidently insane with terror, had tried to escape their rocky dungeon only to be struck down immediately upon leaving the cave, even before his second foot fall.

Many of their company lay dead out there, killed by a frightening and terrible enemy. Only those that had immediately dropped their ill-gotten gains and ran swiftly to the caves had survived. However they were now trapped and some feared the caves were not only a prison, but also a tomb. The thought that perhaps their fallen comrades were the better-off was slowly becoming popular amongst the survivors.

That was definitely the view of one young man, barely out of his teens, who sat alone in a darkened corner. He had never been so terrified and now despair was ensnaring him. He had made up his mind to make a run for it and if he died, he died. It was better than this slow torture. The youth tried to stand but his trembling limbs would not allow him, and he fell heavily against the cave wall and slid to the floor. An anguished cry built in his throat but he stifled it, lest his fellow gang members should beat him.

The boy shivered in the dark, his thoughts as cold as the dank cave. He hated. He hated the rich. He hated his privation. All he had known was poverty and servitude and he hated those he held responsible, especially his parents. Why did they have to be peasants? Why couldn't they be rich landowners? Why must he spend his life in back breaking toil for a master? He wanted to be master of his own life, to make his own way.

He remembered leaving his master's fields, without a word to anyone, with only the clothes on his back, a knife and a lust for wealth. He had quickly thrown his lot in with a gang of thieves, succumbing to the lure of easy riches and, better yet, the opportunity to exact revenge on the objects of his hatred, the snobs of the aristocracy. Besides, it had promised to be a much more exciting and adventurous life than working in the dirt.

Indeed at first all went well with plenty of booty to split amongst themselves. The best of all, he discovered, was that he was able to avenge his sense of inferiority. Watching these fat, arrogant and condescending men of power writhe beneath his knife had been more pleasurable than the fruits of a Jericho brothel.

But yet here he was, cowering in a cave, hounded by a ghostly enemy. It was as if God had turned on him and declared his life forfeit.

The past couple of hours had changed everything though. He had wanted to be wealthy but now he had nothing, not even his knife which he had thrown away in his panic. He had wanted the soft comfort of a bed but now he had nothing but cold rock to lie on. He had wanted to satiate his hunger with exotic fruits and meats but now he was starving.

He had wanted respect but now there was nothing but contempt. At last he realized with great sorrow that hate, his hate, had led him here.

"Why did I not listen to my father?" the despondent man whispered to the gloomy cave. "Did he not counsel me against this? My own arrogance has brought me here to this foul hole surrounded by foul men who have committed foul deeds."

"I deserve this end I know, but even so—I do not wish to die with these criminals in this forsaken place. Oh God, forgive me of my foolishness. I thought I could depend on my own strength and wits and where am I now? Your will be done, if I survive this day I will go home and seek the forgiveness of my master and my father and I will again honor my parents as you have commanded."

The young man then rose and walked to the mouth of the cave. Morning had come. He watched with his fellow captives, some whimpering loudly, as a man and woman made their way along the road. They soon passed from sight but nobody dared to follow because before them stood an army, its soldiers and chariots bathed in blue fire, the horses rearing and pawing the earth, kicking up chunks of rock. Several chariots had taken up positions directly in front of the cave, the drivers holding their spears and swords threateningly. Without hesitation and to the consternation of his former comrades, the young man stepped out of the cave and smiled as he made his second foot fall.

Chapter 6

"Bethany! Praise God, our journey is all but over," Joseph said elatedly and playfully patted the donkey. Bethany was a small village on the southeastern side of the Mount of Olives where the Judean wilderness grudgingly gives way to manicured olive groves and pastures. It had been a long night and day and they were relieved to once again be amongst civilization. Instead of flocks of sheep though, the hillsides surrounding Bethany were dotted with small dwellings made of tree branches.

The Feast of Ingathering had begun and as part of the celebration, the faithful had built booths in which to dwell in memory of their ancestors' journey out of Egypt and into the wilderness.

A group had gathered along the roadside ahead. They were staring at a nearby hill from where a good deal of commotion, yelling and cursing was emanating. A naked man was running between tabernacles, scattering the horrified occupants by throwing rocks and his own dung at them, ripping the shelters apart and finally tossing the sticks and branches into the air.

Women and children fled in panic while a number of men rallied together and gave chase. Their attempts to subdue the man met with painful failure because though small and wiry, the man had the strength of many. He snarled, bit and clawed at the hapless men until they finally retreated; bitten, scratched and bruised and complaining that the man must be demon possessed. The wild man perched himself on a sharp stone and started laughing hysterically. After a time he quieted and began studying his hand as if he had never noticed it before. To the revulsion of all those watching, he furiously started to rip off his own fingernails. He used the blood from his wounded fingers to draw obscene figures on the stone.

He looked up from his masochistic foray to see a gathering of pilgrims staring at him in shock and disgust. He leapt up on the rock and began cursing and blaspheming God. He hurled vulgar insults at them and then cackled maniacally. Knowing it would be foolhardy to try and drive the little man off, the fathers and husbands chose instead to move their loved ones away from who they thought was a crazed, demon possessed individual.

Joseph and Mary were among those trying to move away but too late, the putrid smelling man, in the middle of a blasphemous rant against God abruptly stopped and stared directly at Mary. He seemed to study her as his head swayed back and forth, oblivious to the spittle oozing out of his mouth. Without warning he charged down the hill directly at Mary. Joseph moved quickly to place himself between the man and Mary, grabbing his adz from his satchel while doing so. The crowd fled before the man as he ran down the hillside to the road where he abruptly halted his charge. He stood for a moment jerking and twitching as if he was being stung by a swarm of hornets. Mary kept her face away from the man but to her horror he began to chant in a high pitched, squeaky voice, "Mary, Mary, Mary." The crowd continued to back away from the man, leaving Joseph and Mary isolated. Several murmured amongst themselves as to why this creature had singled out Mary but no one made a move to help. The man shuffled toward Mary, completely ignoring Joseph and the adz in his raised hand, his blood-red eyes never leaving her. "We know you, Mary," he hissed and flung himself at her. Mary screamed and Joseph swung at the man's head only to miss entirely. Joseph looked up to see the man soaring away through the air as if he had been grabbed from behind and yanked away. He landed with a sickening thud, blood pouring from two gaping holes in his chest the size and shape of donkey hooves.

Shaken by the encounter, Joseph and Mary quickly gathered their belongings and fell in with the hundreds of other pilgrims heading towards Jerusalem. Their fellow travelers kept pointing at them and whispering to each other but otherwise Joseph and Mary were left to themselves. Gratefully, they in due course crested the Mount of Olives and beheld a wondrous sight. Across the Kidron Valley was the Temple, its limestone walls glimmering in the afternoon sunlight. The hills around Jerusalem were also dotted with thousands of tabernacles and tens of thousands of believers from all parts of the known world. The road was swollen with merchants and farmers, wagons and animals. The air was alive with sound; music and singing, laughter and an occasional argument. The air smelled of smoke from cooking fires, food and sweat. It was an awesome spectacle to behold and even after their trying and tiresome journey through the wilderness, the couple found themselves newly energized and joyful.

The road leading in to the city gate was lined with government officials and police. Tax collectors seemed to be everywhere as well as those hired to carry out Herod's census. Several prostitutes were busily flirting with a small band of Roman soldiers as Mary passed by. One of them started making indiscreet overtures to Joseph only to recoil in shame after receiving a wounded look from Mary. Joseph, pretending not to notice, guided them through the gate and along the street that would take them to the south entrance of the Temple. There, Joseph intended to leave Mary in relative safety and to go in search of a room and a midwife for her.

The street ran along the base of the Temple court wall which rose forty feet above Mary's head. "It is so immense," Mary said, craning her neck upward. "Our good King Herod must be proud," she stated with no small amount of sarcasm.

"You are becoming a skeptic," Joseph chuckled. "We are blessed to have such a place to come and worship the God of Abraham but the king built this for his glory, not God's."

* * *

"Jesus Barabbas, it is time." Barabbas was impatient to prove himself. He had been a petty thief for most of his young life but now he had a cause, a destiny.

He owed his life to his new mentor, Rimmon. This man had once caught him stealing but rather than throw him in the public prison, he explained to Barabbas as to how his talent could best be used. He could make up for his sinful past and honor God by helping rid Judah of the Romans and their insufferable sycophants, whether Jew or gentile. Barabbas was an easy sell; the scars on his body and within his mind bore witness to Roman cruelty. He hated them and now he would fight them.

From the shadows of an alleyway across from the Huldah Gates the two conspirators observed the crowd. "Remember my young friend, this is crucial, when the deed is complete don't run. You'll attract attention. Just move with the crowd, blend in," Rimmon warned as he surreptitiously handed Barabbas a poniard. Barabbas glanced at the small dagger Rimmon had slipped into his trembling hand and then quickly tucked it away.

Rimmon smiled confidently. "Relax my friend, it'll soon be over. All will be well as long as you don't forget what you've been taught. We'll meet up at the assigned place. Now be quick, your target approaches."

Barabbas stepped out of the alleyway and mixed into the flow of pilgrims making their way to the steps leading up to the gates. However unbeknown to him, he too was being followed.

His target was easy to spot amongst the crowd. A rich merchant no doubt. The man sang louder—and more badly—than everyone else and made a big show of giving money to the lame and blind wretches lying along the steps. Those nearby looked upon him in admiration.

Barabbas bore in. When he was within feet of the merchant one of the two men following Barabbas broke off and began running for a side street. The other yelled that his purse had been stolen and began gesturing wildly at the man running away. As all eyes, including the merchant's, turned towards the commotion, Barabbas struck, sticking the poniard between the man's ribs and puncturing his lung. The man sighed heavily and fell to the ground silently. Barabbas, pretending to have been knocked over, rolled away from his victim and into the gathering sea of onlookers. He got up slowly and joined the crowd pressing in to see the dying man. When shouts of murder rippled through the throng, Barabbas used the consequent chaos to wind his way unnoticed through the throng of bystanders and quietly slip away.

* * *

Joseph could just kick himself. He knew in the back of his mind he should have headed straight for Bethlehem but his pride clouded his judgment. He thought the Son of God should be born in Jerusalem within sight of the Temple for this was the holiest site in all the land. But, to his consternation, everywhere he turned he was met with failure. There were no accommodations left because of the festival, at least there were none that he could afford, Joseph quickly corrected his self. His search for midwives proved fruitless as well. Joseph gazed up at the sky and figured it was well into the afternoon. He needed to move quick if they were going to arrive in Bethlehem before dark. He had family there who, he was fairly certain, would find a place for them. He went to find Mary.

Mary waited desperately for Joseph to return. She needed to relieve herself but did not dare to leave their donkey and belongings unsupervised. Where there are sheep, there are wolves, she remembered her father instructing. Attempting to take her mind off her discomfort she watched the faithful Jews, singing psalms, ascend the 15 steps to the triple gates. Farther west, people were exiting the Temple by a set of double gates. All up and down the street were pools set up for the ritual baths. These baths were required of all men wanting to enter the Temple beyond the Court of Women. Some could hold one or two persons at a time; others were large enough to accommodate groups of twenty or more, the latter being frequented by those of lesser means.

"Ow!" A tearing sensation rippled across Mary's abdomen. She grabbed the donkey's mane to steady herself and waited for the pain to pass. "This is not good," she whispered to the donkey. The pain eased quickly but Mary knew this was just the beginning.

"Where is my husband?" she demanded of the air. It was then she noticed the singing had stopped. She looked around towards the Temple steps to see a crowd gathering. The unusual silence was soon broken by urgent calls for help and shouts of "murder!" Several policemen ran into the midst of the crowd, violently pushing people aside trying to get to the victim. Mary watched the spectacle for several minutes. Everyone in the crowd was either motionless or moving around to get a better look, everyone except for one man who was walking away from the crowd. He walked with purpose, head down except for jerking it backward every few seconds to look over his shoulder. He's not much more than a boy Mary thought as she watched him stride past her. She cringed when their eyes locked for an instant. His eyes were so cold and black. Mary felt she was peering into the depths of Sheol itself.

"He must be the killer," Mary said to the donkey as fear began to pour over her, like an urn of ice water being emptied over her head.

A large hand grabbed Mary's shoulder and she jumped in spite of herself. "Are you all right?" Joseph asked frantically. "I heard someone was attacked." She nodded mechanically; her mind still filled with the disturbing image of the stranger.

"Tell me what happened, you're shivering as if its the dead of winter."

Mary did not immediately respond, allowing her husband's soothing embrace to calm her. She finally patted Joseph on the arm. "I will tell you later but right now I must go."

"Where, I just got here?"

"My husband, I've been sitting here for hours and I'm pregnant, I need to go," Mary replied patiently but firmly.

"Ah, I understand. Sorry."

Joseph sat on the ground casually watching the crowd begin to disperse as the police moved about the street in search of witnesses. By this time the dead man had already been carried away by slaves, the despondent family following in his wake.

Joseph too felt miserable for he was dreading having to tell Mary of his failure to find a room in which to stay. "I am a fool," Joseph said pitifully to the donkey. The animal blinked its eyes as if to concur. "Who asked you?" Joseph stated indignantly.

"Peace be with, Joseph."

Joseph looked up to see a large man standing over him. "Shaaph, my friend, how are you?" Joseph jumped up and was immediately crushed in his friends embrace. "Still winning all of your wrestling matches?" he asked after regaining his breath.

"But of course. When a man enjoys what he does, he excels and I excel at causing pain," Shaaph laughed. He was several inches shorter than Joseph but stocky and strong as an ox. "I see the Sicarii have struck again," he said, suddenly serious.

"Sicarii? What or who are the Sicarii?" Joseph replied, taken aback by Shaaph's odd remark.

"They are not much more than rumor, a whisper on a breeze, but just as dangerous. I move in many circles, Joseph, not all of them are of a proper and friendly nature. These people are bent on ridding Judea of Romans and all who pledge fealty to Rome."

Shaaph studied some men standing nearby for a few moments and then continued, keeping his voice low so that only Joseph could hear him. "The dead man, his name was Ocran. He was growing fat and wealthy providing goods to the Roman garrison at Antonia. Food, wine, pleasure. Understand?"

"Yes," Joseph replied hoarsely. "Are you part of this group? You speak quite knowledgably."

"No, but as I said, I move in many circles. I know things and I am trusted not to speak of them. You are the most righteous man I know and therefore I know you will be discreet concerning our conversation. Listen to me; I too pray for the day the Romans leave but these Sicarii, I fear their methods will do more harm to us than the Romans."

"You there!" Shaaph and Joseph looked to see two policemen approaching them. "Did either of you witness the stabbing?" one of them asked curtly.

"No," Joseph replied immediately. "I only arrived after everything happened."

"How 'bout you wrestler, see anything?"

Shaaph conjured up his most affable demeanor. "I am but a humble subject of his greatness, King Herod. It would be an honor to assist in such a grievous manner but tragically, I was busy shepherding my family to the market. These are perilous times as you well know."

"Do not patronize me you buffoon," the policeman retorted menacingly. "Where is your family now?"

"Sadly, they are in the market place spending my money."

"You mean *my* money you son of dog," grumped the policeman. "We are watching you, wrestler, mind that you don't stray outside the law." He fixed Joseph with a stern look and then stalked off in a tirade of creative vulgarities.

The two friends watched the policemen cross the street and shoo away several kids poking at the drying pool of blood left behind by the dead man. Joseph rounded on Shaaph, "And what was that all about?" he asked quizzically. "Spending *his* money?"

A mischievous grin crossed Shaaph's face. "I wrestled one of their policemen, a big man blessed with the intellect of sheep dung. Our friend here must have bet against me. Never—bet—against—me."

Joseph felt something warm enclose his hand and was heartened to find that Mary had returned.

"And who is this?" Shaaph said with a broadening smile. Joseph introduced Mary and Shaaph to each other.

"I see you have already been blessed," Shaaph said happily after noticing Mary's condition.

THE TRAVAIL

"You have no idea," Mary replied with a giggle.

"Joseph, you scoundrel, I thought I was your friend. You never mentioned you were married."

"My apologies, but we were a bit busy with the police, weren't we?" Joseph replied defiantly.

"What police?" Mary inquired. Shaaph confessed to their questioning by the police. In return, Mary shared with them what she had seen.

"It does not surprise me," Shaaph said after hearing Mary's story. "It is said the Sicarii prefer to recruit the young and unsettled. Now then, let us move on to more pleasant discussions," Shaaph continued in a light voice. "I am sure you are here for the festival, where are you staying?"

Mary looked at Joseph expectantly.

"I haven't been able to find a place to stay," Joseph admitted contritely, his face flushing. "There is nothing available, especially nothing suitable for Mary. Do you know of anywhere?" Joseph asked hopefully of Shaaph.

"Oh Mary, it grieves me deeply that I have nothing to offer you. My own modest home is filled with my wife's family, most of whom I don't even like."

"Then we shall make for Bethlehem, I have some family there," Joseph said quickly. He was touched by his friend's deep concern and felt bad putting for him on the spot.

Another bout of labor pains ended all discussion. Shaaph accompanied them to the gate and then bade them well, promising to check on them in a few days.

Joseph escorted Mary hurriedly out of the city and to the road that led south, across the valley of Hinnom and towards Bethlehem. The valley of Hinnom was a dreadful place. It was not only the city's garbage dump and sewer but served as the place where the carcasses of dead criminals and unclean animals were brought to be cremated. The fires for cremation were never extinguished; they burned even on the Sabbath. As they trudged past a local potter's field, Joseph studied the filthy smoke from the fires as it rose and hung above the valley like a tattered black curtain. Joseph remembered his father telling him stories of the atrocities and wickedness committed by ancient kings in this very place and how in those times the Israelites had turned away from the true God and began worshipping Molech and sacrificed their own children by burning them alive. The priests of Molech would beat their drums loudly so fathers and mothers would not hear their children's screams. Joseph couldn't get Mary away from this evil place quick enough.

Chapter 7

Sounds of cheering echoed through the hills. Levi was putting on an exhibition of his marksman skills for the younger shepherds, using his slingshot to hurl rocks at tree trunks, piles of stones or whatever else the boys would challenge him to hit.

"I found a hyena skull," cried a little red-haired boy excitedly as he scurried down an embankment to join his friends. He proudly held the prized possession above his head as he carried it over to a large stone where he, with great ceremony, delicately set it down while the others looked on eagerly.

Levi had four rocks left. He grabbed the smoothest and flattest one and loaded it into his sling.

After assuming a proper throwing stance he began whirling his slingshot in a circular motion, increasing its speed with each rotation until it was merely a blur. Focusing intently on the hyena skull, Levi let go the leather thong allowing the missile to run true to its target. The skull erupted in a splash of bone with shards and splinters flying in all directions. Levi smiled broadly and happily accepted the praise of his fellow shepherds as they danced and whooped.

"Why are you rascals not attending to your flocks?" Joha berated. The young shepherds stopped dead in their tracks and hung their heads, embarrassed that the old man had managed to sneak up on them again. "You boys know better, especially you Levi. Sunset approaches and with it comes danger."

"It is my fault, Joha. The little ones were bored. I was just about to send them on their way," Levi said as maturely as possible, hoping to deflect some of Joha's rancor. He looked around at his fellow shepherds hoping for some show of support however they just stared back at him suspiciously. Apparently his "little ones" remark did not go over well with them.

"Bored?" Joha bellowed. "Humph. What do you know of being bored?" Joha asked, staring at each one in turn. "Levi, how long have you been a shepherd?"

"Six years."

"And you there, how long?" Joha said pointing a gnarled finger at the freckled faced, red-haired boy.

"Two years," the boy replied meekly, obviously uncomfortable with being singled out.

"How long was Moses a shepherd?" Joha asked taking on the tone of a rabbi.

"40 years," they replied in unison (this issue had come up before).

"Do you think Moses ever complained of being bored?"

"Nooooo," they replied in unison again.

"Exactly."

"But David killed Goliath when he was not much older than Levi here," a boy complained.

"David did not kill Goliath," Joha replied patiently.

"But you told us the story....ouch!" The boy rubbed his backside after receiving a blow from Joha's staff.

"And shame on you for not listening," Joha reprimanded. "Did David not say to Goliath, *'This day God shall deliver you into my hand'*? David gave the glory to God when he struck down Goliath and then King Saul's army drove off the Philistines. This is a lesson all of you would do well to remember." Joha then shooed them out into the gathering dusk to watch over their allotted flocks.

Before Levi could leave, Joha turned to him, "Be careful what you wish for lad. I wanted excitement too and ended up conscripted into King Herod's army. He forced us to fight against our own Jewish brothers."

"Why?" asked Levi. "I thought the *Romans* were our enemy?"

"Sadly, that is not the case. Herod owes everything he has to the Romans, to Caesar. He surely will not bite the hand that feeds him."

"So what happened?" inquired Levi incredulously.

"Many years ago, I was just a young man then obviously, there was a rebellion. It started in Galilee and spread to Judea."

"It figures the Galileans would start the rebellion," Levi cut in. "They are such a backward, ill-tempered people."

"That may be so but they paid dearly for their impudence. The rebellion embarrassed Herod for he had told Caesar to his face that he could control the Jews. So, he gathered his army, including me, and marched north into Galilee. The slaughter was horrible. Male, female," Joha paused, his eyes moistening, "or child....didn't matter, all were put to death. When we returned to Jerusalem it was found out that some of the rebels and their families were hiding in the Temple. They were caught, dragged into the street, and butchered." Joha shook his head slowly as if to rid himself of this hideous memory. "Herod is a terrible man and he will kill to protect his rule. Pray Levi, pray the Messiah comes soon. Pray he will drive out the Romans the way David drove out the Philistines."

The watchtower stood high on a hill overlooking the countryside around Bethlehem. Because of the commanding view it provided, it was used by the shepherds to keep watch over their flocks of sheep and for protection from marauding bandits. It had the shape of a goat's horn with the pointed end lopped off. The tower was ancient, having been rebuilt many times over the centuries. Parts of the tower wall were constructed of quarried stones; other parts were made up of field rocks stacked one upon another. It was built over one of the many caves that dot the hills around Bethlehem which made it the perfect place to bring ewes that were about to give birth. Within the cave were a number of stalls which were kept ceremonially clean by the Temple priests who oversaw the birth of each lamb, for these were not ordinary lambs, these were lambs to be used for Temple sacrifices in Jerusalem.

According to the shepherds' folklore, this was Migdal Edar, or "the tower of the flock" referred to by the story of Israel and Rachael when she died giving birth to Benjamin. And though it had been constructed for humble purposes, the tower had been used by the kings of old as a stronghold to defend against invading armies; in times of turmoil and unrest, the cave had provided secrecy and concealment for plotting rebels. The history of the watchtower was of little concern to the two lonely figures struggling slowly along the steep crooked path

THE TRAVAIL

leading to its entrance way. One was leading a heavily burdened animal, the other was carrying a child in her womb and they were desperately seeking sanctuary for the time to give birth was upon her.

Joseph and Mary squeezed through the narrow opening into the cave below the tower. Joseph guided Mary to the nearest stall where he threw off his tunic and laid it on a bed of old straw. He then helped Mary sit and propped her as comfortably as possible against the wall. He rushed back out to retrieve their provisions, unfastening and removing satchels and bags as quickly as possible. The donkey brayed at the rough treatment.

"I don't want to hear it," Joseph muttered. He had hoped Mary could make it into the town of Bethlehem where they had a good chance of finding hospitable shelter but she could go no further, the baby was coming soon and she could no longer walk or ride. Getting into the tower had sapped her remaining strength and will power. She had to stop. There was no more time.

Just as he was about to re-enter the cave he stopped and began searching through one of the packs, pieces of cloth and tools were flung onto the ground as he dug deeper into the satchel. With a triumphant grunt Joseph held aloft the object of his search, a small oil lamp. He began walking towards the entrance, stopped, picked up the hodgepodge of implements that had fallen out of his pack and then headed back for the entrance.

"Joseph, you must hurry! The pains are coming!" Joseph, flustered, quickly picked up the packs and tried to run through the opening. He bounced off and fell backwards. He lay on the ground winded by the impact. Eventually the pain seeped into his stunned mind and Joseph let out a yell followed by several moans. Not only did his head and shoulder hurt but he was pretty sure a rather large rock had lodged itself in his back. Something wet and gooey smacked him in the face. Joseph opened his eyes to see the donkey's face inches from his own.

"Laughing are you?"

Another cry from Mary brought Joseph back to the task at hand. He jumped up, his pain and humiliation suddenly forgotten, and scooped up the oil lamp and a flask of oil and this time carefully entered the cave.

With the sun setting, the pittance of daylight coming through several fist sized holes in the tower wall was almost worthless. Joseph set about the familiar task of lighting the oil lamp. Joseph could hear Mary breathing heavily. He filled the lamp from the flask using his fingers to ensure he had poured the correct amount. He stuffed a piece of wool in the narrow end of the lamp and then raked together some straw with his fingers. Using several small rocks he carried on him, he began striking them together to create a spark. After several minutes Joseph succeeded in building a small fire and used the burning straw to light the lamp. The gloom of the cave was beaten back some by the tiny flame, the light provided being just enough for Joseph to make out an old wooden stool and small table along the opposite wall and a stone manger towards the back of the cave.

Joseph reached out for Mary's hand and looked up at her face, the feeble glow of the lamp reflecting off the sweat beading on her forehead. He expected to see a frightened girl but instead, to his astonishment, he saw a determined woman, her eyes shining with resolve. Mary gasped as her abdomen once again convulsed and burned with pain. Her mouth fell open in a scream. Joseph thought his fingers would break if she squeezed his hand any harder.

When the contraction had subsided Mary took some deep breaths and pointed into shadows, "Joseph, I need that stool to sit on."

Joseph brought the stool over to Mary and helped her up. He tried to smile confidently as he dabbed the sweat from Mary's face.

"Mary, I know nothing of child birth. This baby was to be born in Jerusalem, in the shadow of the Temple, and with the assistance of midwives and even musicians to announce his birth. What can I do?"

Chapter 8

One by one the shepherds guided their flocks into a patchwork of crude paddocks erected at the base of a hill which was nearby to where Joha had set up their camp. Once the flocks were safely corralled into their designated paddocks, commands were issued to collect firewood and to prepare the evening meal. Levi looked hopefully to Joha for an indication that a ewe could be slaughtered to eat but Joha ignored him. Bread cakes and figs again, Levi moped.

After the less than satisfactory meal the seven shepherds settled in for the night. Within moments the boys were engaged in a lively game of five-stone[8]. Joha sat nearby quietly observing the game, listening to the boys' playful banter. He relished their innocence. Would his heart ever be unburdened of his sins he wondered hopelessly? As a young man he had been forced to kill fellow Jews in the name of the king. As the years went by the horrors he committed vexed his mind and soul. He wanted badly to make amends for his sins and so he vowed to himself that when his duty to the king's army was completed he would pursue a life of peace. Once released from the army, Joha hurried away from Jerusalem towards Bethlehem to become a shepherd for it was in the hills surrounding that little town that the sheep specifically raised to serve as sacrificial animals for the Temple were pastured. The priests took him in and trained him in the care of these special animals since it was crucial that these animals which were destined to be sacrificed remain unblemished and free of sickness. Ewes were watched closely, those that tended to stray or failed to get pregnant were soon fattened and slaughtered. The priests were vigilant overseers; they even oversaw the birthing of lambs. Prior to lambing season the stalls within the cave below the watchtower were made ceremonially clean. Ewes that were about to lamb were brought into the watchtower so they could be free from the stresses of weather and predators. The new born lambs were immediately wrapped in swaddling clothes to prevent any injury.

Joha got up and moved over by his friend, Nebajoth, the stiffened muscles in his legs fighting against his every step. Nebajoth was slow of mind but had the physical strength of an ox and though not quick witted, he possessed an admirable passion for the safety and well being of his charges. Although the younger boys would never admit it, they always felt safer when Nebajoth was nearby. While the boys played the two men watched the sunset; its display of darkening ribbons of peach and rose colored light inspired Nebajoth to retrieve his flute from a goatskin bag and begin playing. As he played Joha felt his pains and worries melt away. Oh so brief, he thought, but the respite was welcome indeed. Joha often remarked to anyone that would listen that his friend could play better than the sons of Jeduthun. There was a time when Joha could play competently as well but his once nimble fingers were now crippled however he could still sing (a bit raspy though, to which Joha would freely admit) so when Nebajoth began playing one of his favorite psalms Joha sang along and loudly.

Nightfall was coming on quickly and the red-haired boy had first watch. He slung a skin of water over his shoulder and trudged off into the gathering dark. He looked back longingly at the camp; he could hear the boys bickering over some alleged trickery. He took a circuitous route around the paddocks using the remaining slivers of light to check for strays. Satisfied all was well, the boy sat down next to a tree. There was a narrow thicket of low brush and thorn trees between him and the camp but he could still see the glow of the fire through the tangles of branches.

He took out his flute and played a song that Nebajoth had been teaching him. At times his small fingers would stumble over each other and he would play a note so poorly that the sheep grazing nearby would stop and take notice, or so the boy imagined. When he finished he lay back on his tunic and stared up at the stars and worried if Levi would leave him out here by himself all night again. A fresh breeze began to blow which the boy appreciated, the air having been stagnant all day. The air gently flowing across his skin felt like the loving caress of his mother's hands on his shoulders. He sniffed the air, it smelled of spring flowers, an unusual but welcome change from the pungent smell of sheep which typically permeated the air.

The sound of a Nebajoth's flute came floating on the wind; it was one of the psalms he played often. The boy closed his eyes in order to focus on every note Nebajoth played. Rivers of color flowed and spiraled around in his mind while the aromatic breeze seemed to come and go with the rise and fall of Nebajoth's melody. "Peculiar," the boy whispered right before sleep finally took him.

"Child, wake up." The red-haired boy felt somebody kicking his foot startling him awake. He was momentarily confused but after remembering where he was, anger and shame swept over him. Levi had caught him sleeping he thought guiltily. To assuage his guilt he allowed his anger to rise at Levi for calling him a child.

"The arrogant dog," the boy hissed.

A light mist had moved in while he was nodding off, filling the low areas between hilltops with pools of white. The boy looked around but there was no one to be seen.

"Levi? Is that you?" the boy said fighting to control his trembling voice. He did not want to give Levi the satisfaction of knowing he was a little scared. He walked around the tree he had been leaning against holding his staff out in front him, ready to hit anything that moved.

"Child." The boy whipped around to see a figure seemingly take shape out of the mist.

"Who are you?" said the boy quickly realizing this was not Levi. "Are you a thief?" he pursued while waving his staff threateningly.

"Would I have bothered myself to wake you if I were a thief?" replied the man patiently. "I wish to speak with your friends; would you please show me the way?"

Despite the starry night the swirling mist made it difficult to navigate and the boy soon lost his way.

"I'm all turned around," the boy finally admitted to the

stranger. "The others let the fire burn down so I'm not sure which way to go."

"Continue on, child," the stranger replied out of the gloom. The path is before you." The red-haired boy glanced up at the sky, located the North Star and set off again. Though he was heartened by the stranger's confidence, still he couldn't help feeling a little irritated at being called a child.

As they drew near the camp the boy began to realize that the land about him was growing brighter which, the boy thought, was odd since sunrise wasn't for many hours, in fact the sky above him was still dark. He studied the ground before him and what he saw bewildered him. Fingers of mist were seeping into the plants and bushes, even into the very ground itself. About him nettles and brambles wilted and died; thorn trees evaporated in wisps of smoke. Dumbfounded, the red-haired boy hurried on to the camp only to find that his fellow shepherds were already astir, having been roused by the unusual light. The light was like that of lightning in both color and intensity, beautiful but yet terrible to behold. The strength of the light then grew rapidly, overwhelming the shepherds who, one by one, fell to the ground, and cried out in fear.

"Get up, do not be afraid," a voice commanded gently. Levi uncurled himself from the fetal position and perfunctorily spit some dirt out of his mouth. The voice was unfamiliar but yet reassuring and authoritative like that of his father's. He stood and stared wide eyed at the stranger in their midst. He was like no man Levi had ever seen for his tunic was the color of new cotton and his skin shone like bronze. Could this be an angel, Levi thought?

In the sky above the shepherds, thick clouds boiled and

THE TRAVAIL

rushed like storm driven seas against rocky cliffs. Before them, all manner of plants and trees radiated light which produced colors as rich as the most precious of jewels; leaves and grass took on shades of the green jasper and emerald, the branches of trees and bushes shown with the color of black onyx and brown topaz. Even the patches of bare ground sparkled like fresh snow beneath a clear winter sky. The once dull cream colored limestone rocks and outcrops had become a dazzling display of pinks, browns and yellows of agate and beryl. Even the lowliest bush had become as colorful and majestic as an almond tree in spring.

"Amazing, isn't it?" the stranger said. The shepherds' only response was to nod dumbly.

"Excellent, now listen," the stranger said smiling broadly, no longer able to contain his excitement. "I bring you good news of great joy that will be for all the people," he said sweeping his arms in a wide arc. "Today in the town of David a Savior has been born unto you; he is Christ the Lord." The angel's words caused a sudden warmth to envelop Joha's body. He was at once comforted and energized as the thought immediately occurred to him that this was no man standing before him, but an angel of the Lord. What a blessing, he thought, that the Messiah had been born in his lifetime. Joha felt the burdens on his heart driven away by this new wonderful sense of hope, just as thirst is driven off by a cool drink of water.

"And this will be a sign to you," the angel continued. "You will find a baby wrapped in swaddling cloths and lying in a manger."

Immediately peels of thunder crashed throughout the

heavens, the din was of such magnitude that the shepherds felt the ground shifting beneath their feet. And then diving out of a swirling mass of clouds that was rolling down from the north, came the Cherubim arrayed in garments of blue, purple and scarlet. They flew quickly to and fro across the horizon like dragonflies racing amongst the reeds of a river bank, their wings beating the air with a sound like that of rushing water.

The Cherubim assembled in the sky above Bethlehem, forming into a great ring around the city like guards surrounding a king. As one they each drew a flaming sword from jewel encrusted scabbards hanging from their waists and hovered quietly above the town. All was quiet for a short time, the shepherds shook like leaves on a tree. With the sound like that of a thick curtain being rent in twain, the clouds rolled apart. Beyond the opening lay a great city, shining with a brilliant light, appearing as if the sun was rising from its very center. The city was enclosed by towering walls of jasper and gates constructed of pearl. The gate in front of the shepherds swung open followed immediately by the blast of countless trumpets, the sound of which, Levi was quite certain, would cause ears to bleed. A multitude of heavenly beings then poured forth out of the gate marching upon a sea of glass, led by an angel dressed and armored like a great warrior. The host of heaven paraded past the shepherds towards Bethlehem, trumpets blaring all along the way. Once the procession had reached and enveloped Bethlehem it halted and all became still.

Joha looked about at the mighty gathering and felt incredibly puny, like a crawling insect gazing up from the floor of Jerusalem's hippodrome. While marveling at the awesome sight before him, a gathering of emotions fought for control within his bosom. Should he shout for joy, Joha thought earnestly, or flee in fear? Either way his ability to keep control of his bodily functions was quickly becoming disturbingly suspect. Being a devout Jew, Joha was familiar with the scriptures and therefore knew of angels. He had long tried to imagine what they looked like but was now discovering that his pitiable mind was no match for what he was seeing before him right now. Most of the angels resembled the one that had delivered the message to the shepherds of the Savior being born but amongst them were a variety of others including several that were the color of glowing embers. He also saw one being with many wings and a face like that of a man. The creature was closely accompanied by three others; one looking like an eagle, another resembling an ox and the last having the visage of a lion. There were still others that did not so much look like angels but appeared as plain men clothed in the whitest of raiment with crowns of gold upon their heads.

Levi's heart was thumping rapidly; it felt like it was seconds away from bursting out of his chest. With difficulty he pulled his eyes from the vision before him to gaze at his fellow shepherds, if for no other reason than to assure himself he was not standing there all alone. He was stunned by what he saw; his mentor, Joha, no longer looked like a worn out old man but stood erect with the demeanor of a king, his once dull eyes now sparkling like blue sapphires. Levi then turned his attention to Nebajoth who had the fascinated look of a child given a new toy. Levi then looked to other side of him where the boys were standing. No longer did they appear as mere shepherd boys with unkempt hair, dressed in soiled clothes but had now taken on the mien of princes, even their typically bruised and scratched skin appeared unblemished.

Music began playing, softly at first, becoming louder as more instruments added their voice to the song. The flowing melodic sounds of harps and lyres was punctuated by the crash of cymbals and underscored by the pulse of beating drums. The music continued to crescendo as the heavenly ensemble played. Joha felt the sounds flow around him like eddies in a stream, the beating drums and timbrels resonating through his bones and sinew. A chorus of angels began singing. Their voices intertwined in a masterpiece of harmony that was as pleasing to the ear as the touch of the finest silk was to the skin.

The Levite priests singing in the Temple sounded like crying babies compared to this, Joha thought as he listened to the angels sing:

"Glory, Glory, Glory to God in the highest,
Glory, Glory, Glory to God in the highest,
Glory, Glory, Glory to God in the highest,
Glory to God in the highest,
Glory to God in the highest,
Glory to God in the highest,
Glory to God in the highest, and on earth peace to men,
Peace to men on whom his favor rests."

The choir fell silent but the music continued on, building to a climax of sound composed of trumpets, horns and other musical instruments whose sounds were wholly unfamiliar to the shepherds, the music becoming so powerful that they felt tossed about like boats caught in a tempest. After a final trumpet blast the music quickly faded away and the shepherds collapsed to ground like puppets whose strings had been severed. Levi was the first to sit up and look around, his ears ringing, the campfire was licking lazily at the night, above him the stars shone brightly, their celestial light reflecting off of the wool of the sheep, making the flocks appear as clouds hugging the ground. A pair of wolves howled in the distance.

"Let's go to Bethlehem," Levi heard Joha say excitedly, "and see this thing that has happened, which the Lord has told us about. And then we will wake the city with the news!"

"No one's going to believe us, Joha," Levi replied. "We are just shepherds, who will give an ear to us?"

"Some will, the righteous will. It is written in scripture that the Lord is close to the brokenhearted and will save those who feel crushed and alone."

"The angel said the baby was wrapped in swaddling clothes and lying in a manger. Which manger? How do we know which one?" Levi wondered aloud.

"I know." All eyes turned to look at Nebajoth. He was looking in the direction of Bethlehem, his cheeks glistening with tears. "When I was a child my father patiently taught me this verse, 'And thou, O tower of the flock, the strong hold of the daughter of Zion, unto thee shall it come, even the first dominion; the kingdom shall come to the daughter of Jerusalem.'"[9]

"Follow me," Nebajoth instructed. His friends happily obeyed and fell in behind him, marveling as they walked about all that they had seen and heard.

Epilogue

"It looks like the Lord has blessed us again," Joseph remarked casually waving his hand towards the low clouds scudding across the sky.

"How so...?" Mary responded after a moment. She had been whispering softly to her baby boy and kissing him on his cheeks.

"It's not raining and in fact, we may actually get to Jerusalem and home without getting wet."

A few minutes later it started to drizzle. Chagrined, Joseph looked at Mary and shrugged his shoulders. Mary smiled but really didn't care. She had her baby Jesus and that is all that mattered. They were taking him to the temple to be consecrated to the Lord as the law required. It had been 40 days since Jesus had been born and 40 days since she had been able to mingle with people, she was happy to be out of the house no matter what the weather.

After entering the Temple Joseph left Mary to purchase an animal for sacrifice. He came back shortly thereafter with two doves.

"What is wrong?" Mary asked after noticing the irked look on his face.

"I'm having one of those days, I guess. I thought I had brought enough money to buy a lamb for the dedication but I didn't. Prices have gone up so the two doves were all I could afford," Joseph complained. "The priests are allowing the holy Temple to become more and more like a market place. It disgusts me."

The doves were handed over to a priest and once sacrificed, Mary and Joseph headed for the Temple's exit gates however, before they could leave the court they were approached by an elderly man. Joseph recognized him immediately since he had seen him many times before praying in the Temple. His name was Simeon, a man known for being virtuous and a dedicated servant of God.

"Sovereign Lord," Simeon began as he reached for Jesus. Joseph nodded to Mary, assuring her it was okay. Simeon took Jesus in his arms and continued in a loud gravelly voice, "As you have promised Lord; now you're letting me, your servant, depart in peace. My eyes have seen your salvation, which you have now prepared in the sight of all the people; a light for revelation to the Gentiles and for glory to your people Israel."

Simeon gently laid Jesus back into Mary's awaiting arms. While doing so he said, "This child is destined to cause the falling and rising of many, and a symbol that will be spoken against, so that the thoughts of many hearts will be revealed." He then looked at Mary sadly. "And a sword will pierce your own soul too."

As Simeon was speaking a prophetess named Anna came forward, joy radiating from her face. She took one look at Jesus and immediately began praising God and telling all who would stop and listen about the child and the coming liberation of Jerusalem.

Many Jews and Gentiles heard Anna's words that morning, unfortunately though, few listened. And even fewer understood. Men of stature and education dismissed her words as the ranting of an old woman but one rough looking man, lurking within the shadow of a portico had been listening intently and knew her words to be true.

Ranting? The arrogant fools…these words are portentous, even dangerous, the man thought to himself. He stepped down from under the shade of the portico and into the gloomy morning light, his colorful robes billowing in a strong breeze which was whipping through the courtyard.

When the king hears about this that child will die, the man thought sadly. It was hard to imagine a baby of such humble origins challenging a powerful king but his duty was not to question but to report what he had seen and heard. His duty though could wait; he had other more pressing business that required his immediate attention. With that thought he quickly exited the courtyard but not before taking one last look at the couple and their child. He was perplexed by their ordinary appearance, they looked nothing like he had imagined.

Endnotes

[1] A surveying instrument used by Roman surveyors.
[2] These were soldiers who possessed specialized skills. Their expertise in their respective fields such as surveying allowed them to be exempt from the more tedious and dangerous tasks other soldiers were required to do, such as ditch digging and rampart patrol.
[3] Leviticus 23: 26-28 NIV
[4] Luke 1: 46-55 NIV
[5] 1 Samuel 8: 11-18 NIV
[6] Psalm 127: 3-5 NIV
[7] Psalm 23 KJV
[8] A game similar to "Jacks".
[9] Micah 4: 8 KJV